Janice Hutchings

Bohemian Summer

novum ▲ pro

This book is also
available as
e-book.

www.novum-publishing.co.uk

© 2016 novum publishing

ISBN 978-3-99048-282-7
Editor: Chennai Publishing
Cover photos:
Kevin Eaves, Chris Lofty, Monkey
Business Images | Dreamstime.com
Cover design, layout & typesetting:
novum publishing

www.novum-publishing.co.uk

Acknowledgements

For my novel Bohemian Summer, I thank the Plymouth Writers Circle for their tireless critiques and advice. My chiropodist, Martin Hunt, for his faith in my imaginings. My long suffering partner, Ian, when querying certain passages and what he terms "IT SUPPORT". Derek, my Jack Russell, who'd found it all incredibly boring and a waste of time. And last, but not least my late husband, Clifford, who made everything possible.

CHAPTER 1

It was that time of year in the picturesque village of Nettle-bridge, when swifts, with the air heavy with a scent of roses mingled with the fragrance of honeysuckle borne on a summer breeze, were preparing to leave for their wintering grounds.

Iris Blackmore stood by the open casement, drinking in the morning air. A dark-haired woman, petite in stature, with piecing blue eyes, in Harry, her husband's opinion, a force to be reckoned with.

Her mind still absorbed with memories of the previous evening, she pondered.

What had obsessed her to suggest such a meeting, to resolve the ongoing issue of the gypsies, and such a seemingly unsolvable one on everyone's lips? Once again, she experienced that same feeling of hopelessness when picturing the unrelenting animosity of the villagers amassed in the church hall. On such a wet and windy night, she had been pleased to see such a good turnout.

At first, the evening had gone true to plan, each point of view noted and amicably discussed, that is until halfway through the evening. The door swung open to reveal the rain-coated figure of Mildred Marsh, a known gossip and troublemaker. From then on the atmosphere in the room changed dramatically, the Colonel who up until then had been quite subdued had become quite belligerent. He like Mildred, harboured an intense dislike of the gypsies, it was as if her presence, had given him the impetus to voice his hatred of them. Voices raised, in the chaos that ensued, many of the villagers made for the door. Iris for once wanted no part of what would have been a relatively successful evening. Reluctantly, she had left a disgruntled few with the Vicar and Mildred Marsh still arguing the toss by the empty stage.

Iris filling the kettle mused. True there had been a valuable ring stolen from the then artist's studio in the village, from the boundary walls of the churchyard, a number of coping stones unaccounted for, but that was nearly a year ago.Then as now in her opinion, the finger of suspicion had unjustly pointed at the travellers. At that time, causing no trouble at all they had been encamped on a rough piece of commoners land on the edge of the village where one hardly ever saw them. Neither did she blame Farmer Brown for profiting from the extra revenue, by letting out a field of which he had no apparent use.

The Colonel or Squire as he liked to be called, had become an embittered and lonely old man and somewhat of a recluse, since his wife's death. Arrogant and self-opinionated refusing all offers of help, his presence in the village created an embarrassed silence. He now habitually disappeared for hours on end in the woods, but no-one knew where nor questioned why.

The kettle whistled filling the small kitchen with steam. Iris filled a large earthenware teapot with boiling water. She tucked in a stray strand from her otherwise tidy hairstyle, and, then straightened her floral wrap-over. The kitchen was untidy and not up to her high expectations. She was forever picking up after Harry, had reprimanded him on many occasions, but he either would not or could not see it her way. She took a cursory look around. Discarded newspapers, spillages, half-empty milk cartons, you name it, hopefully, Charlie would not take a leaf out of his father's book. When they had first married, everything had seemed so perfect, but now every day was so humdrum.

An empty beer bottle caught her eye and picking it up she scrutinized it, before tossing it into the waste bin. Sweeping up cigarette ash and dog ends, she wished Harry didn't smoke so much, better he'd come with her to the meeting, still he didn't get drunk like some men, she should at least be thankful for that.

Take the Colonel for an instance, living in that big house, all by himself. He had never been the same since his wife's death and at such a young age too. T'was in a car crash, wasn't it? Iris searched her memory.

And then Charlie, their only son, Harry's slovenly behaviour up until now had had no adverse effect on him, had it? Of course, he got up to all sorts of mischief but then boys will be boys!

Iris looked up on hearing the click of the latch.

The door creaked open. 'You're up early, how's that?' Harry raising an enquiring eyebrow, wiped his muddy boots on the doormat.

'I thought I heard something.'

'That damn fox was after the hens again. I wish I'd had my shotgun.' Mopping his brow with a grubby handkerchief, he sat down heavily on a kitchen chair.

'Did it get any?' Iris asked, handing him a mug of tea.

He shook his head.

'Well, that's alright then, I'm glad to see you wiping your boots.' She added, with a hint of sarcasm in her voice.

Harry running his fingers through blonde hair, now tinged with grey, gave a look of disapproval, soon to be replaced by a mischievous grin. 'What about me breakfast, woman,' he said, slapping her lightly on the backside.

'You behave yourself!' Iris exclaimed, smiling at his audacity. 'Keep your hands to yourself!' She lit the gas and cracked eggs, thinking as the bacon sizzled in the pan, Harry's so endearing, he never bears a grudge.

'Smells darn good to me, where's Charlie?' Harry indicated the empty space at the table, '… Not down yet?'

'Really Harry, where else would he be!' She dished up and handed him his breakfast. 'It's the start of the school holidays.'

'I suppose we won't see much of him then, still he could help out a bit.' He studied her face. 'You look tired.'

Iris stretching across the kitchen table helped herself to another slice of buttered toast. 'I couldn't sleep.' She yawned and rubbed her eyes.

'Couldn't sleep?' Puzzled, he asked. 'Why?'

'It was that meeting, you know…' Iris felt a sense of relief when unburdening herself, 'The meeting in the village hall last night.'

'I didn't hear you come in.' Harry reaching for the teapot, poured himself another mug of tea, and taking a slice of bread, wiped his plate clean. 'Guess I must have drifted off to sleep.'

'Probably, anyway it ran on far too late and the Colonel was upset.' She grimaced.

'Upset.' Slightly confused, Harry asked, 'What about?'

'Harry, do keep up!' cried Iris, exasperated with his lack of interest. 'You know those confounded gypsies.'

'Oh that, is that all.' Her husband gave a smug smile, then pulled a face. 'The old man's got it all out of proportion, I blame you and the villagers for pandering to him.'

'He's not the only problem.' Iris sighed. 'There's that interfering Mildred Marsh, she's always stirring things up.'

'She was there then?'

Iris nodded, soulfully.

'Now we're on the subject, I saw the Colonel this morning passing the gate. He was with his old retriever. To me he looked like he didn't have a care in the world. He was making his way along that narrow footpath into Peckham Woods. I wondered where to, especially at that time of the morning. Still it's none of our business is it?' Harry getting up, slipped on his working jacket and stepped to the door. He turned and smiled. 'See you tonight, love.'

Iris her hand on the sill, watched his retreating figure. Through the open window, the fragrance of a rambler, carried on the breeze, tainted by the odour of silage, wafted from a neighbouring field.

Iris thought of the Colonel. His attitude intrigued her. Where was he now? She wondered. Why was he rarely seen? Had he something to hide? She mused. To be sure, the Colonel was indeed a man of mystery.

⁓≈⁓

In an otherwise cloudy sky, a ray of sunshine broke through highlighting the tip of the church spire. Iris on her way to the village shop paused by the church gates to check her shopping list. With not a soul in sight she looked up when hearing the ting of a bicycle bell, just in time to see the Vicar rounding a bend in the lane. Brakes screeching he drew abreast, the old bike shuddering to a halt.

It was a sturdy-framed bicycle but needed a lot of attention. She eyed it sceptically, as he dismounted. 'The bike's seen better days,' she said, appraising its rusty exterior.

'It seems none the worse for wear, the tyres haven't perished.' He smiled, touched by her concern, but quite unperturbed. 'I found it in an old potting shed in the vicarage garden; someone must have left it behind.'

Relative newcomers, the Rev. Ralph Watson, his wife Maria and daughter, Julie had soon settled down in the rambling old vicarage next to the church, and in no time had won the hearts and minds of the villagers. Some even said, 'He'd charm the birds off the trees.'

The Vicar glanced at his wrist watch. 'You're up early.'

'Yes, so my husband said just now. I thought I'd make an early start, I've some shopping to do.'

'I'll walk along with you, that's if you don't mind.' He grasped hold of the bike's handlebars.

'That will be nice,' said Iris, her mind elsewhere. This time, she told herself. I mustn't forget to pick up some washing powder.

Outside the shop front, Iris bid 'Goodbye.' She stood and watched, shaking her head in disbelief, as the Vicar wobbling precariously, pedalled down the fore street past Sid Evan's Bakery.

~~✥~~

One could always rely on picking up the latest gossip in the Nettlebridge General Store. The proprietor, Mr. George McDonald, a stocky built, ruddy faced, congenial man of forty, was proud of his establishment and considered himself a pillar of the community. A confirmed bachelor, he gave the impression that everyone could expect a welcome on the mat on entering his store. The shop front had recently had a face lift with a 'Wet Paint' Sign urging passers-by to take care. And now with the morning sun glistening on its windows, and green coat of paint dry, really looked quite impressive.

As usual, Iris before entering it's interior was drawn to the adverts in the side window. This morning, wiping away the condensation, she scanned the board, her eyes darting from one card to another. 'Pup needs loving home, Tel. etc. After ...,' hopefully Charlie would not see that. 'Part-time cleaner, flexible hours, Tel. …,' handy to know; 'Lost, Ginger Tom answers to the name of Marmalade,' how appropriate, someone must be upset; 'Newspaper Round, preferably a young boy …' applicants must be enthusiastic. She'd mention this to Charlie. But what was this? Another notice almost shouted out at her, in large black capitals, it read, 'NO GYPSIES SERVED HERE.' So much for George's so-called hospitality, it obviously had its limits.

'I wonder what the Vicar will think of that?' she mumbled.

The shop bell jangled as Iris stepping in distracted a number of villagers grouped around the counter, their eyes focused on Mildred Marsh.

'As I was saying, and I'm not one for gossiping unnecessarily.' Surrounded by a rapt audience, still in her ascendancy, Mildred stopped abruptly, as heads turned towards the door. Somewhat ruffled, she smiled indulgently on seeing Iris, and then carried on. 'As sure as I'm standing here, as large as life I saw him …'

'Saw who?' asked Iris, baffled by such intensity.

'Why the gypsy who else, really Iris who do you think I meant?'

'Perhaps the Colonel?'

'I saw him this morning, the Colonel that is.' With all eyes levied in her direction, Emily Woods, a frail old spinster dithered.

'How was he?' asked Iris, aware of her discomfort.

'Just the same.' Emily snapped open her purse. 'Yes, I could do with some loose potatoes, I've enough here,' she muttered, after counting the change. 'Just the same I think …'

'Doesn't matter what you think.' Mildred's eye started to twitch.

'Don't you dare speak to her like that,' snapped Iris, staring at Mildred, 'She's a right to her opinion.'

'I myself don't think it's right and proper to be discussing the Colonel,' responded Mildred truculently, holding her gaze, while Emily coughing nervously fiddled with her string bag.

Iris had never liked Mildred Marsh. They hadn't seen eye to eye on several occasions. She remembered the time when Mildred had found Charlie's ball in her garden and wouldn't give it back; and then again Guy Fawkes Night when a banger had exploded

12

right next to her porch. She'd sworn it was Charlie, although it wasn't, and Iris had known why. Mildred had it in for him because she, Iris, was the only one who stood up to her. Others not so brave, avoided any such confrontation. A big woman with steely grey eyes, her ample bosom heaving when pointing the finger at some unsuspecting villager or child, she generated fear, a person not to be trifled with, even the Vicar, relatively new to the village, found it difficult to engage in conversation with her.

'Good morning, Ladies, I'm sorry to have kept you.' George McDonald having emerged from a back room straightened his apron. 'I was in the stockroom. Now who's first?' He caste an enquiring eye.

'You were telling us about the gypsy.' Undeterred, one of the group, turned to Mildred.

'Yes, well not now, I've lost my thread, I've other things to think about. When I've been served,' she looked fixedly at George, 'I'll be on my way.'

'You were first?' He raised an eyebrow.

'Of course!'

'You've got other things to think about, have you?' cried Iris. 'If that's so, if you feel so strongly about the gypsies, why were you so late coming to the meeting last night?'

With a face like thunder, Mildred flounced out slamming the door behind her. A rapt silence prevailed, the bell jangling noisily, as swinging from side to side.

The first person to speak was George who having momentarily covered his face with his hands, was now audibly mouthing the words, 'My door, my door, the hinges.' Much to their surprise, with his fist he thumped the counter, uttering loudly as tongues started to wag. 'Ladies, Ladies enough of this, this is a place of business, now who really is next?'

Iris coughed and catching his eye asked, 'I just wanted to know if the position had been taken for the paper round? I was thinking of my Charlie he …' Conscious of a certain amount of hostility, she blushed, hastily adding, 'I'm sorry to have butted in, it really isn't my turn.'

'My dear, there's no harm in asking.' replied George, feeling a modicum of pity. 'The Newspaper Round, I should have taken the card out of the window, how remiss of me. The round was taken only a while back by …' He paused and scratched his head, 'by, now who was it? My memory is not as good as it used to be.' Frowning, his countenance lightened. 'Now I remember, it was the red-haired boy, Gerry Pearce, the milkman's son. What is it you wanted Emily? You were next I believe. Potatoes? Certainly, I'll weigh you up some, they were fresh in today.' At that moment, Iris could have sworn he winked at her.

In a lighter frame of mind, Iris clutching her purchases left the shop, thinking as she went on her way, he wasn't a bad old stick, after all.

෨෧

CHAPTER 2

In the heart of the woods, an owl twit-twooed. The retriever pricked his ears when hearing a sudden movement, the scent of which lingered with a fluctuating breeze, on all fours watchful he lay, sniffing the air.

Colonel Clifford Hardwick in a grassy copse positioned himself comfortably on a fallen tree trunk to drink in a freedom of fresh air and sunshine. He found it good to sit alone in a silent solitude, broken only by a babbling brook and birds on the wing. He no longer relished village life, but would have preferred a rudimentary hut in the woods, had age not hindered him, with only the wildlife for company.

In such a tranquil setting, a shot rang out, breaking the spell. Oscar, wild-eyed, barking frantically, scampered down the path out of sight.

'Damn the gypsies!' The Colonel muttered under his breath, 'Poaching, I'll be bound … What!' He mopped his brow with a red-spotted handkerchief.

In the ensuing silence, lulled by the murmuring waters, memories came flooding back. An image of his wife, as a young woman on the brink of life. A chance meeting that had changed his life, now without her, a bleak outlook.

Unashamedly, tears trickled down his cheeks, a nostalgic train of thought, broken by a muffled bark. The old man opened his eyes as Oscar, brown eyes glowing with pride, laid a trophy at his master's feet. 'Good lad,' the Colonel murmured.

Oscar's tail twitched. To show the old man he heard, the dog raised his grey muzzle.

The Colonel, a burly man, generally showed little emotion. At one time a leading light in the village with his wife at his side, he had partaken in all facets of village life as Chairman of the Parish Council.

Now alone, he felt isolated, misunderstood and very much on guard, only letting the mask slip on occasions such as these with Oscar, his dog.

Up early that morning in the grey dawn, his dog at his heels, he'd threaded his way down the narrow woodland path to his leafy haven to find peace of mind.

He often questioned himself about his newly enforced nomadic existence. Was he going mad? Weren't the gypsies nomads too? He knew not nor cared what the villagers thought about his attitude, but condescended to make a rare appearance such as the one last night in the church hall, when it suited him.

The weather wet and windy, no sooner through the door, as expected, his eyes had met a blur of faces in a noisy crowded room. Trying to be inconspicuous, he had quietly taken a seat in the back row. Half way through the evening, the door had swung open, all heads had turned. Framed in the door none other than, a drenched to the skin Mildred Marsh. He had heard that she was a trouble maker, that the villagers took measures to avoid her, but felt an empathy for wasn't he too misunderstood.

In no time evoked by her dogmatic views about the gypsy encampment, a heated argument had developed, the atmosphere in the room charged, a once orderly meeting out of control.

Amidst voices raised in anger, blindly, he'd unceremoniously pushed past all and sundry in a bid to beat an hasty retreat. The rain had cleared, and outside on the steps in the cold night, unleashing Oscar, he had been happy to be alone.

On the edge of the clearing, with Oscar at his side, the Colonel stood and looked down at the world he loved, the world he would have preferred to live in alone and abandoned.

The hill sloped gently below him, a rough stony track joined by a fork leading to the Gables, its stately portals and ornate façade basking in the noon day sun.

A ray of sunshine fleetingly lit up the gnarled trunk of an ancient oak, just like his memories with it's passing nothing but a dream. A muffled whimper with a bark jerked him back to reality. The old man smiled. He bent down and patted the retriever on the head. 'Come on, Old Boy,' he said. Straightening up, he shouldered the shot gun. 'Let's go home.'

At the same time, out all night poaching, with little to show but a brace of pheasants slung over his shoulder, the gypsy trudged along the rutted road where not far away blue smoke wisped from the gypsy encampment.

◦◦◦◦◦

One could not fail to notice 'The Gables.' A rather pretentious red-bricked building in it's own grounds, situated on the outskirts of the village. A mansion, for that's what it was, now housing but a single occupant. It's many windows glinted in the mid-afternoon sunshine, like so many eyes, looking out onto ornate manicured lawns set on either side of a wide gravel path, sweeping down to rusting wrought iron gates.

In his study, the brocade curtains partially drawn, Colonel Clifford Hardwick puffing on a half smoked Havana, poured himself a generous whisky and soda. From a side table, he picked up the 'Sporting Life' and scanning it's contents, eased himself into his favourite armchair by the hearthside.

'Nothing much here,' he muttered, placing the paper on his knees, he closed his eyes. Vaguely aware of the paper falling onto the tiger skin rug, he was back in India. Imaginary smells assailed his nostrils of spices in the bazaars, the faint musty smell of dry water buffalo dung, dust and decay. He pictured himself as a young officer striding past the harbour walls to the sounds of cracked trumpets, drums, and shouts from the water carriers.

A privileged child, the Colonel brought up in the foothills of the Himalayas, in the days of the Raj, had been the only son of wealthy parents. Idolized by his father, Charles, a tea plantation owner, Clifford Hardwick had led an idyllic life. At an early age, he accompanied his parents on the obligatory social circuit: cocktail parties, polo and tennis matches, and tiger shoots in unbearable heat.

The family's carefree life style came to an abrupt end shortly after Clifford's eighteenth birthday. He joined the Indian Army. He soon found favour with his commanding officer and rose rapidly up through the ranks.

In no time, Clifford received a commission and, as luck would have it, spotted his future wife. He was on his way home from the Chandrapore Club when he paused by the tennis courts to watch the young women throw themselves at the ball.

Then he spotted an angelic being. Could she really be that beautiful? He rubbed his eyes. Was he seeing things? She was tall and slim, silky blonde hair cascaded over her shoulders. Her long shapely legs were bronzed by the sun.

He was spellbound, and stayed until the end of the match, a turning point in his life.

Seated on a bench, in the half light, aware of his interest, with no intention of leaving the others, she'd glanced in his direction. Taking this as an invitation, he had joined her. In the next few hours, it wasn't so much what they said as their awareness of one another, or so it seemed to him at the time. The evening air was thick and warm. She'd drawn closer to him, laying her head on his shoulder, as they watched the sun set in a final blaze of glory. Later, in a starlit sky, the moon in a layer of cloud, as it emerged, they held hands, in the moonlight beside a silvered stone Buddha partially entwined with red strands of bougainvillea, this the first of many chance meetings, mainly contrived on his part.

The Colonel waking with a start, sat up and rubbed his eyes, as the heavy oaken study door creaked, prised open by a wet nose. Padding across the room, Oscar nudging him, rested a wiry head on his knee. The old man smiling, patted the dog's flank. The carriage clock, its hands pointing to four o'clock, chimed the hour. 'Was that really the time?' It hadn't seemed long since he'd left the leafy haven of the woods, partaken of the cooked meal left warming in the oven on his return, read his housekeeper's note.

He watched, as with a gentle breeze, the roller blind lifted, sending a shaft of light, which rested fleetingly on a silver framed photograph of his then young wife.

Just like his memories of Nicola … nothing was tangible or permanent, but with it's passing nothing but a dream.

Nicola Davenport, the only daughter of Brigadier Ernest Davenport, had been the talk of the cantonment. Her coquettishness had led to a number of indiscreet affairs with wealthy men.

On many a sultry evening, Nicola could be seen seated at the long bar surrounded by male admirers. Her slender fingers, perfectly shaped painted nails, holding a long silver cigarette holder. She would throw her head back and laugh outrageously at something somebody had said. The memsahib raised their eyebrows, tongues wagged. Some chose to turn a blind eye to her overblown behaviour, others simply retired gracefully. The Brigadier and his wife often excused themselves on some pretext.

'She's like a loose cannon,' one officer was heard to remark to guffaws of laughter, 'But a nice one.'

'I heard you … A loose cannon I'm not! For that nasty remark, you horrible, horrible, little man, you can get me another drink. Yes, a Singapore Sling.' Her voice slurred and discordant she'd swung around on the bar stool and burst into song, 'You're the cream in my coffee.'

Bored with their company, lurid stories and vulgarity one evening she'd found herself distracted by a solitary figure. A young army officer, not much taller than herself, with tousled brown hair, seated at the far end of the bar scrutinizing a broadsheet he'd placed on the counter. After a while, he'd risen stretched his arms and yawned. Intrigued, she'd watched him fold the paper, drain his glass, and leave the room. She known immediately he was the one, that they were destined to meet.

But distant storm clouds gathered on the horizon. In the bazaars, remote villages, and countryside, the news spread like wild fire.

What with trade sanctions and with Ghandi stirring up the natives, clashes were inevitable and with the uprising, an air of gloom hung over the cantonment. Interest in Nicola waned. Instead of going to the Chandrapore Club she'd started playing tennis, telling all and sundry she chanced to meet, 'I'll fire at random, should they attack!' She'd changed, becoming at times quite subdued and serious, even more so after meeting Clifford.

Clifford said very little, but when he voiced an opinion, she hung on to his very word.

When he announced, quite out of the blue, 'I think we should get married.' She readily agreed.

With the onset of border skirmishes, with his parents Clifford had witnessed the subsequent bloody aftermath, an ordeal that had taken the toll of their health and ultimate demise. Clifford discharged from the Army, with the honorary rank of Colonel, together with his young wife, took the first convenient boat back to England. Nicola now pregnant, and never one for roughing it, with all the change and upheaval suffered a miscarriage in the process.

Until their eyes had alighted on the little village of Nettlebridge, each had felt like refugees in a foreign land. That is until out driving in their newly boughten Austin A35 on that memorable sunny summer's day they'd spotted the 'For Sale' sign. The red-bricked mansion on the outskirts of the village, had drawn them like a magnet, willing them to buy it. And before long they had settled in with a new acquisition, a puppy dog, aptly named Oscar.

At first evoking a certain amount of curiosity and conjecture, in no time at all the villagers' doubts were dispelled, and the Colonel and his memsahib were soon to find themselves as popular as the Vicar and his wife would in the ensuing years, that is until the accident.

Since then, the Colonel the villagers had known, was not the one they knew now, the one they hardly saw.

Many an hour, with inclement weather or when he felt at odds with the world, if truth be known, Clifford Hardwick could have been found languishing in the depths of his saggy armchair. A comforting blaze in the open fireplace; the flames mirroring a far-away look in his hooded eyes, within reach a cut-glass whisky decanter; a cigar butt smouldering in an ashtray, on his knees an open photograph album.

He'd turn each page; with a smiling image of Nicola, recapturing so many memories, tears welling up in his tired blue eyes when he'd thought of what might have been.

It wasn't as if he had particularly wanted children, perhaps it was simply his male ego working overtime. Why hadn't he listened to her at the time, when there had been such recriminations? She'd always been highly strung and spoiled, and like him had led a pampered life. But with the shock of seeing her parents slaughtered, now a stranger, locked in a black tunnel of despair, not the gay and carefree Nicola he had first met and loved. When she had become pregnant, he had been glad, thinking having a baby to love and care for would dilute or solve the problem. But with it's loss, her attitude had hardened, she'd shown no grief, but had avoided him, going out on her own. She'd stressed on a number of occasions that she had no intention of having any more babies, and had not wanted any in the first place. To the villagers they had appeared a loving couple. Then one particular sultry summer's day, things had come to a head.

Nicola in one of her rages, had been drinking most of the afternoon. She had driven off in the car. And that was the last time Clifford had seen her alive.

Only Mrs. Symons, the Colonel's elderly housekeeper, understood the hidden traumas, the insecurities, and unspoken words of a somewhat subdued, frightened but proud old man. The offer of a hand of friendship, would have been unthinkable as their easy going relationship with 'no questions asked' would have been broken. In his own time, she would think, if he wants to talk, I'll be there for him.

The Colonel picked up his crumpled edition of the 'Sporting Life', smoothed it out and folded it carefully. In the subdued light, the tigers yellow eyes glared sightlessly up at him as he placed it back in it's rightful place. Hungry, protesting, his stomach rumbling, stubbing out his cigar, he drained the last remnants of the whisky. A muffled bark jerked him out of his apathy, sitting in front of him, Oscar raised an expectant paw. The old man smiled when struck by the thought. 'A real friend, a faithful one.' He bent down and patted the retriever on the head. 'Come on Old Boy,' he said straightening up and making for the door. 'We mustn't keep Mrs. Symons waiting.'

CHAPTER 3

It was quiet in the village, and beginning to get warm, when just ahead of him, Charlie spotted Mildred Marsh. His heart sank, and then tempting fate, he increased his pace; drawing abreast, he caught a glimpse of her face.

Mildred totally unaware of him, apparently had a grievance. He slackened his pace. Ma always told him to avoid her if necessary, only to speak when spoken to and then answer in a polite manner. Why bother, he thought, when visualising her flushed angry countenance, he didn't even like her. But deep down he had to admit that Ma was right, even when tempted at random, as now, to throw a stone at her greenhouse and smash glass panes shining in the mid-morning sun. He was glad to see her with the click of her garden gate, hurry up the path to her front step, unlock the door and go inside.

Once past her thatched cottage, on the edge of the village, Charlie soon found himself in open countryside. Behind him, a cluster of higgledy-piggledy backyards, gardens and cottages, drowsing under a cloudless sky, now barely visible, almost a mirage, ahead as far as the eye could see a network of narrow lanes, leading off in various directions. These in his time, he had explored, but today already bored with his own company, he wandered aimlessly.

With the sun gathering strength, Charlie stopped in a dusty lane, and squat on a large flat stone, beside a farm gate. Wiping beads of sweat from his brow with a grubby handkerchief, he saw through it's bars, a wide expanse of pastureland, running alongside it a stream sparkling in the sun, beside it cattle drinking, others chewing the cud or lying down.

Hot and perspiring, just as Dad always did, Charlie knotted his handkerchief and placed it over the top of his head to protect it from the sun's rays. His tongue was dry, and he felt thirsty.

He pricked up his ears, as a dog's bark broke the silence. Probably a farm dog, he thought, tethered up in one of the farmyards. He wished he had a dog, like Oscar, the Colonel's retriever, or even an old mongrel. His big blue eyes misted over at the thought. Ma was always stopping him from doing things. He would go behind her back, find a stray, smuggle it into the back shed, and feed it on scraps. No-one would know.

Further down the lane, on the other side, ignoring a weathered sign on which had been scrawled 'Keep Out … Beware of the Bull', he climbed over a gate and dropped down to the other side. But for a scattering of sheep, he hadn't seen a bull or even a cow. Fearful, in case there was one around, his heart pounding, holding his breath when envisaging a thunder of hooves, he scanned the field.

Up on the skyline nestled a farmhouse and outbuildings. No-one seemed to be around, but to him, the farmhouse windows glistening in the sunshine seemed like eyes, that watched his every move. In the distance, he heard the sound of an unseen tractor, and on hearing the drone of a light aircraft, cupping his hands over his eyes, watched it until merely a speck in a wide expanse of blue.

Charlie seized again by a feeling of unease, had just decided to turn back, when he caught sight of the dog. Riveted to the spot he watched it. At a distance, it was running at speed down over a grassy incline from the farm. But what sort of dog? He shaded his eyes to get a clearer image. As far as he could tell, it was a mottled grey colour with long legs. Perhaps it was the farmer's dog. It started to run in a zigzag direction between the sheep, scattering them in all directions. A shot rang out. By the gate, he stood transfixed, holding his breath, willing it to escape. As it neared the brook in it's frantic flight for survival, came another shot, a bullet ricocheted and the canine fell.

'No … no! 'e can't be … 'e 'ain't' Charlie, his mind in a daze, his surroundings a blur, cried out as half running, half stumbling across the field towards the motionless body. 'I 'ate all farmers… I 'ate 'em … I 'ate 'em!' Tears moistened his eyes. 'How could 'e an wi' a gun too, 'e wosn't doin' any 'arm.' A thought occurred. What would he do if it was injured, how would he patch it up?

By a thick clump of grass under a sycamore tree, the dog laid still and silent, a large male, with the appearance of an Irish Wolf-hound. His heart beating rapidly, Charlie approached the animal cautiously, at first not knowing what to expect. Eyes closed, fur matted with blood, the dog gave no sign of life.

As if on a mission, finding an empty carton amongst the long grasses bordering the stream, Charlie scooped up some water.

'Drink this.' He lifted the carton to the dog's muzzle, his grubby fingers smoothing the wiry fur.

At the sound of his voice, the animal stirred, lifting his head, he licked the moisture spilling out.

'Is that yourn? … I'll 'elp e' if 'e wants me to.'

The voice seemed to come from the tree. Charlie looked up to find partially concealed in it's leafy arbour a boy, with the darkest eyes, almost as black as his unruly mop of hair. Charlie gasped. The boy grinned at his reaction. 'Wot, ain't 'e seen a gypsy afore?'

'No, I, I don' think I 'ave.' stammered Charlie, quite taken back, but trying not to stare. None of his classmates or anyone he could think of looked like him. Olive skinned with a gold ring in one ear, barefoot, about the same age as himself, the gypsy boy wore a loose tunic and dirty trousers and tiring of Charlie's silent scrutiny asked, 'I said, 'Is 'e yourn?' He pointed to the dog.

'No 'e ain't, I wish 'e wos though.' Charlie replied dolefully, 'E's 'urt some and I don' know wot to do.'

As if aware of his concern, the dog raised his head, and whimpered when making a feeble attempt to get up.

'If 'e ain't yourn, then 'hose is 'e?' The gypsy boy asked, slightly puzzled.

'Dunno.' Charlie wrinkled his brow. 'Didn't 'e 'ear the shots?'

'Oh that.' responded the gypsy, somewhat flippantly, 'I saw an' 'eard everythin' from up 'ere.'

'But … but don' 'e care!' Charlie was astounded. Rubbing his eyes, he leant over to take another look at a now very subdued animal. 'e's breathin' alright,' he remarked,' but 'e ain't wearin' a collar.'

'Tis only a stray I suppose,' the boy commented, matter-a-factly, 'Us 'ave plenty runnin' round. They tag along when us is on the move, some 'itched to the wagons, t'others loose git rundown or somethin'.'

'Don' 'e like dogs?' asked Charlie, 'I really wish I 'ad one.'

The gypsy boy shrugged his shoulders. 'I suppose them's alright in their place, that's if 'e bothers 'bout 'em at all.'

'Oh …' Somewhat perturbed, Charlie lapsed into silence. He thought of the Colonel. He went everywhere with Oscar.

'Youm quiet, anythin' wrong?' Now in turn, the gypsy was scrutinizing him.

'Nothin.' Charlie kneeling down, fondled the dog's head.

'Wot's 'e called?' the boy asked.

'Charlie Blackmore, I comes from the village.'

'Well Charlie meet Marco. Yer really upset 'bout that dog, ain't yer, … can't think why.' Marco grinned. 'Tell 'e wot, I best go'an git Mario, 'es me Dad, 'e knows 'bout these things.'

Charlie watched as Marco, just like a circus acrobat shinned down the knotted tree trunk from his perch, high up in the branches. Although more agile than himself, he was surprised to find himself taller than Marco, although he was beginning to realise that the gypsy had the upper hand.

'Stay 'ere, don' 'e go wanderin' off.' Marco standing at the foot of the tree trunk, looked quite formidable. Sensing Charlie's anxiety, he chuckled. 'Else the gypsies will git 'e.'

With Marco gone, the dog at the sound of Charlie's voice, opened his eyes and looked up at him, sad brown ones but intelligent, partly obscured by tufts of hair. Once again he attempted to get up, but weak and still reeling from his ordeal fell back, sighing he closed it's eyes, as if resigned to his fate.

Charlie in the shade of the tree, sat on the bank, dangling his legs in the stream. In the limpid shallows, a crab emerging from behind a rock took fright, as Charlie thrashing his legs sent rivulets of water, rippling across the surface, stirring up the sediment. There was not much he could do but wait. The dog had not moved and as far as he was aware asleep.

After a while, Charlie somewhat apprehensive when hearing in the distance, a murmur of voices and the creaking of wheels, got up to take a look. He crossed his fingers, and murmured, 'Please let it be Marco and not the farmer.'

'I said us wouldn't be long, didn't I? Us gypsies always keeps our word.'

Charlie relieved on hearing once again, the familiar voice, shading his eyes from the sun, saw Marco and supposedly his father.

'This is me Dad … said Marco with a smug smile. 'But 'e can call 'im Mario like I does when I wants, can't 'e.'

The gypsy gave a condescending smile.

It wouldn't have crossed Charlie's mind to call his father by his Christian name and even if it had he wouldn't have dared, but if Marco's father didn't mind, there wasn't anything to worry about.

If he had met Mario under any other circumstances, Charlie would have either hidden or run away. To him Mario looked like a pirate, like those in his picture book of 'Treasure Island.' Just like Marco, Mario was olive skinned with a golden ring in his ear but wearing a tattered cap. His black opened-necked shirt over which he wore an unbuttoned faded embroidered waistcoat, partially exposed a sunburnt black hairy chest, to Charlie a fearsome sight. Unlike Marco he wasn't barefoot, but wore old trousers and rather muddy boots.

'Cat got yer tongue?' he said in a deep voice, equally as interested in Charlie with his blonde hair and blue eyes.

'I … I … don' know what to say.'

'Then say nothin',' said Mario, gradually warming to what he thought was a shy sensitive boy. 'Now us must see to the dog.'

The old wheelbarrow groaned under the dog's weight, as the three of them carefully manoeuvred it through the long grasses to the gate. Now and then Charlie caste a sidelong glance at Mario's profile, the Romani's mouth set in a firm line in his endeavours to overcome any obstacles. Quite out of breath, they eventually reached the gate.

'My the dogs a dead weight, and wi' that wheelbarra an' all …' Mario commented, addressing no-one in particular. 'still us'll soon 'ave 'im fit an' on 'es way.'

'But, but!' protested Charlie. He looked and felt hot and flustered.

'Yes son, what's wrong?' The gypsy raised an enquiring eyebrow.

'Nothin'.' Charlie cringed under the gypsy's gaze.

'That's alright then,' said Mario, puzzled by his attitude.

'He wants a dog of 'es own,' explained Marco. He puffed out his chest. 'I told 'im, us 'ave plenty.'

'Is that all.' said Mario. 'Us 'ad better git goin' then, I've a 'orse to shoe.'

സ്ലൈ

The piercing whistle shattered an otherwise tranquil setting of sun drenched lush pasture land, where wild thyme and other aromatic herbs grew in profusion, their heady aroma wafting in the summer air. In one corner of the field, a trilby hatted dark skinned man, in an orange shirt, shoeing a horse, looked up as dogs of all shapes and sizes, barking excitedly, converged on the farm gate; with Mario's booming voice, quickly dispersing.

Charlie lagging behind had never seen so many. Collarless in their eagerness, each trying to be first, in their path, scrawny bantams taking flight, they'd almost upset the wheelbarrow and it's precious cargo.

'ave 'e fed 'em, them an' the birds, Marco?' Mario gruff voice rose above the din. A nicotine finger pointed to the bantams. 'Them looks 'alf starved.'

Marco nodded. 'Yea, wi' scrapes as many as I could lay me 'ands on, but the dogs gits 'em.'

'Chain them dogs to the wagon wheels.'

'Can't do that, there's too many of 'em.'

'Chain some, then … Mawnun, Amica on yer way,' the robust Mario, distracted at that moment, by a dark-haired girl driving

28

a dog cart, laden with baskets of pegs and plastic flowers, smiled broadly. A colourful nosegay in her braided hair, she wore an outmoded frilly lilac dress. Her dark eyes shone as coaxing a piebald, out onto the lane.

Marco in passing nudged Mario. 'er wos tellin' me them's 'ardup. Them pegs ain't sellin.'

'Ain't us all.' Mario grimaced. 'Tis 'ard fer 'er on 'er own wi' the abuse on doorsteps an' all. But 'er always got a smile on 'er face, I'll grant 'e that. Best Salvador 'elp 'er out. Make out some cards 'an push 'em in doors fer anythin' folks wants rid fer cash.'

Abuse? Charlie thought of the sign he'd spotted in the side window of the grocery store. Drawn to words, written in large black capitals, he had read 'NO GYPSIES SERVED HERE.' Why? He pondered. Mario and Marco had helped him with the dog, they needn't of.

Just across the field, beside a sunlit stream bordering an outcrop of trees, a brightly clad gypsy woman, wrung out and spread clothes to dry on overhanging branches. She neither looked up nor spoke on their approach, her mind elsewhere. The woman picking up her washing basket made for and climbed up steps into a wooden wagon, from which smoke spiralled from a makeshift chimney. The wagon in this case, painted yellow with black rimmed wheels, as others it's panels highly decorated with birds and flowers.

'Salvador's bin out all night poachin' an' ain't come 'ome yet, last time 'e came 'ome drunk. 'ers in one of 'er moods.' Mario chuckled. 'Serves 'er right, 'er chose the wrong man, 'er could 'ave 'ad me.'

From within the nearest wagon, by which children were playing bouncing up and down on an discarded sprung mattress, could be heard, cries and reprimands.

'Juanita's fallen down again.' Marco grinned.

'Yes son,' Mario grimaced. 'er's small, 'er'll grow out of it.'

'Juanita, what an odd name', thought Charlie, wondering what she was like. But not for long, for the door of the wagon burst open and a little girl in a scarlet dress clambered down the steps.

She had just joined the other children, when catching a glimpse of them her face lit up. As fast as her little legs could carry her she ran towards them arms outstretched.

Half laughing, half serious, Marco placing his hands over his eyes, exclaimed, 'er's runnin' too fast, 'er'll come a cropper, 'er 'ain't lookin' where 'er's goin.'

From the wagon's interior, a loud reprimand broke the silence. 'Juanita, come back 'ere!' A buxom gypsy woman with braided tresses, shiny hooped earrings and wearing a wine coloured dress, emerged frowning, her dark eyes searching the field for any sign of the little girl who had been trying her patience all the morning.

'Juanita! Juanita! Where are 'e, wait till yer Dadda comes 'ome.' Exasperated, her mouth set in a firm line, gathering up her skirts, she laboriously made her way across the field.

In the shadow of a tree, momentarily resting the wheelbarrow, Mario scooped up the little girl and placed her on his shoulder. Aware that the woman hadn't spotted them, with a wry smile on his face, he stood and watched her fruitless endeavours from a distance. Charlie took a look at the dog. A dreadful thought occurred. The dog appeared to be still asleep, but what if he was dead. Mario and Marco did not seem concerned, if anything they had lost interest.

The gypsy woman stopping in her tracks, her cleavage heaving with her exertions, had by now caught sight of Mario pushing a wheelbarrow. He was not alone. Marco and a young boy were with him. She eyed the group curiously, on their approach muttering. 'It's my Mario and our Marco, but 'hose that? And wot's in the barra?'

The old wheelbarrow eventually came to rest with a jolt close to the steps of the wagon. Mario wiped his brow. The dog now awake, it's head hung over the side.

'Poor thing, wot 'appened?' the woman questioned, all thoughts of Juanita forgotten.

'Farmer took some pot shots,' replied Mario. 'Reckoned 'e wos worryin' the sheep. Body's peppered with pellets. Fur's matted wi' blood!' He exclaimed, moved by the shock in Eliza's voice.

She drew closer, her eyes widened. 'Dog's 'ad a narra' escape.' She disappeared inside the wagon. Moments later she emerged with a red plastic bowl, sponge and a large bar of soap, a grey blanket slung over her shoulder. 'Build up the fire, 'usband. Git the kettle boilin'.'

With fresh kindling, sparks flew. Mario wheeled the barrow to the fire, then lowered it to the ground. Suspended from a hook, over the flames, the kettle filled with water from a bucket, boiled. Mario taking the blanket from Eliza, spread it on the grass.

'There, there … old boy,' Eliza whispered in soothing tones, gently sponging down a dog, too weak to resist with a bowl of warm soapy water. Gently, she wrapped him up in the blanket.

'T' will do 'im good to rest, given time 'e will be as right as rain,' commented Mario.

So the dog was alive! Charlie felt a thrill of excitement, perhaps in time it would be his dog, after all he'd found it and Marco didn't seem to mind.

'Well no-one can say I ain't well mannered,' said Mario. He directed his remarks to a rather subdued Charlie who stood awkwardly to one side. 'This 'ere is me wife.' Mario with a flourish, pointed to the woman. 'er answers to the name of Eliza. And this is Charlie, e's from the village.'

'I thought so.' Eliza scrutinized Charlie, drawn as Mario had been to the pale faced, pensive boy with the blonde hair and big blue eyes.

'How do you do … Ma-am?' Charlie extended his hand just like Ma always did.

Eliza threw back her head and laughed uproariously. 'Well I never … I've never been addressed wi' so much respect.' She curtseyed. 'Charmed I'm sure.'

Charlie blushed, as stepping towards him she shook his hand, her eyes dancing with merriment. Directing her gaze at Mario, she gasped. 'e could take a leaf out of 'is book.'

Mario faked a cough and cleared his throat. Taking the lid off a large smoke-blackened, caste-iron cooking pot, and sniffing it's steamy contents, he remarked pompously 'Now with the formalities over, t'is time for the stew, ain't it ready yet, wench?'

'Don' 'e call me wench!' Eliza glared at him.

'And don' 'e whistle when 'e comes into the field next time or 'e'll set the dog's off again.'

Seated on the steps, Marco smirked. He knew Mario would forget.

'Dadda,' a small voice piped up. The little girl who sobbing, had been nestling her head in the crook of Mario's arm, looked up into his face. 'Juanita ain't, all bad?'

He smiled at her and with a grubby finger wiped away the moisture from her tearstained face. 'Not always,' he replied, smiling at her naive and concerned expression. 'Not always,' he whispered in her ear, gently smoothing the silken black hair from her forehead.

The stew bubbled away, carrying with it tantalising odours that made Charlie's mouth water. Eliza with a saucer full attempted to feed the dog, who at first resisted her attempts, although after a while tempted, swallowed a few morsels. Scrabbling with his paws, he tried to get up once again without success, and laying down, with Eliza soothing tones, soon closed his eyes and sound asleep. Needless to say, watching her Charlie's faith had been restored, if Eliza cared for dogs that much, so must Marco.

It was some sort of stew or was it soup, whatever it was Charlie couldn't make up his mind. Seated cross-legged between Marco and Mario in front of the fire, he felt so ravenous, that he soon cleared the bowl. His face now glowing from the fiery heat, although fully replenished, his eyes shining, he looked up expectantly at Eliza who smiled and ladled out some more. It was delicious, a combination of nettles, herbs and meat, maybe pheasant or rabbit. In no time, he was feeling quite relaxed, and closing his eyes, finding it difficult to stay awake, fell asleep.

Sometime later, still not fully awake, Charlie stumbled across the field on Marco's heels. Mario and Eliza watched them from their log seat beside the open fire, Eliza trying to restrain a petulant Juanita. The little girl tugging at her arm wanted to follow them.

The sun blazed down on the gypsy encampment, flinging wild shadows, birds flew from tree to tree, branches swayed in the wind. A kestrel hovered in the turbulent air then plunged from a duck egg blue sky on a unsuspecting field mouse. Charlie watched as the bird, who having gorged its prey, perched on a rock by the stream, was now preening itself, shining each feather with oil until it lay sleek and smooth against it's body. Clean, its plumage immaculate, it lazed in the sun. Like it there would be other hungry shadows haunting the surrounding countryside.

'Charlie git a move on!' Marco now on the very edge of the woods stood watching and waiting.

Charlie soothed by the moving strains of a violin, and the muted voices of travellers at ease, playing cards in the shade of a tree, rolled up his trousers and sat on the bank. Soaking his feet in the glistening waters of the stream he stirred up the sediment. A crab scuttling sideways, found sanctuary under a submerged rock.

∽✧∽

The woodland path normally well-defined and well-trodden was now very nearly obscured by a tangle of overgrown grasses, weeds and wild flowers. In the dim green interior, a network of pathways under a canopy of foliage fanned out in every direction. Birds twittered, taking wing on their approach. Before them on a carpet of dead leaves and pine needles, they could hear the scurrying of little creatures, some unseen to the naked eye. A little way ahead, Marco stopped in his tracks and motioned Charlie to keep still and silent. The sun's rays slanting through the trees picked out the burnished red coat of a fox emerging from a thicket. It stopped, sniffing the air, ears alert, picking up their scent, tentatively lifting a forepaw, it dropped a pheasant from it's drooling jaws. With wild hazel eyes ready to pick out the slightest movement, the fox having retrieved it's trophy, on velvet paws disappeared into the shadowy undergrowth.

'Farmer Brown 'ates foxes … 'e's always laying traps for 'em, says they be too wily … what's wily, Marco?' asked Charlie.

'Dunno.' Marco paused, apparently deep in thought, he screwed up his eyes, as if attempting to make an impression. 'Tricky I suppose, catchin' all them there fowls and suchlike.'

Marco always some way ahead, led the way, not once stopping to answer one of Charlie's questions. He pressed on, his eyes bright when proudly airing his knowledge. Charlie trailing behind, the gypsy boy stomped on further into the woods, passing such remarks as, 'That's not a mushroom, that's a toadstool, 'e can't eat 'em, them's poisonous. Some berries 'e can eat, some 'e can't.'

But … but which is which?' Charlie wanted to know.

As the afternoon wore on, Marco tiring of Charlie's thirst for knowledge distanced himself leaving Charlie behind.

Charlie hurrying to catch him up shouted after him. 'Wait fer me!'

On hearing the sound of Charlie's voice, echoing in the still woods, Marco stopped and looked back. Exasperated he shouted, 'e soon knows … I did, it's wot 'e learns like. Come on slowcoach, stop askin' questions.'

For a moment, Charlie felt rejected and upset, but wanting to please and impress his new found friend, called after him, 'If 'e waits fer me I'll show 'e where the Colonel lives.'

❧

The sun was setting, as Colonel Clifford Hardwick approached the large wrought iron gates finding to his consternation that they were ajar. It was not like Mrs Symons to forget such a trivial gesture, for she was a creature of habit and generally could be relied upon.

Oscar pushed aside the gate with his muzzle and padded up the path, stopping now and then to pick up a tantalising scent.

Now bathing in the aura of the sun's dying rays, the garden had taken on a radiance so breathtaking, that even the Colonel who generally didn't notice such things, couldn't resist stopping for a moment to savour its beauty. The old man taking a deep breath, inhaled the perfumed air, marvelled at the majesty of the setting sun, revelled in its glow, all thoughts of his current loneliness and despondency forgotten. An idyll short-lived with Oscar scratching the front door, trying to gain admittance.

Just like the dog, Clifford Hardwick was beginning to find life difficult to face with all its uncertainties. The Colonel on nearing the steps felt tired and weary. His body and limbs sluggish, an inexplicable feeling, one of foreboding swept over him, so instead of entering, as was his custom by the front door, he chose for some reason to take the side path leading to the back kitchen.

Oscar running on ahead, his ears pricked and senses acute had picked up a scent.

Clifford slowed his pace, then stopped and listened. He could have sworn he had heard voices, albeit muted ones in the grounds, or had he imagined it? At the door, he turned the key and stepped inside. Oscar in his basket, he made his way upstairs.

⟨✶⟩

'Go on then, I dare 'e to show me where tis?' I can't see no 'ouse' Marco eyed Charlie suspiciously. 'Youm making 'im up ain't 'e.'

Charlie was beginning to feel tired and irritable. 'I ain't ...' he rejoined defiantly, 'I ain't lyin' 'e's real.'

'This Colonel ... wot's a Colonel anyway?'

'T'is some sort of soldier. It ain't far now, maybe 'e'll see the chimnee's when us leave the woods,' said Charlie. 'It's a fine 'ouse, a gent's 'ouse.'

An owl hooted as tired and dishevelled, they reached an area where the trees thinned out. In the twilight, they stood looking across darkening fields at the twinkling lights of the village beyond.

'Wot's the time?' asked Charlie, seized by the thought of Ma and the lateness of the hour. She would be wondering where he was and worrying. But he didn't want to go home, not yet.

'I see chimnee's just beyond that there 'illock.' Marco scrambled up the slope and looked down. 'My wot a place! 'E weren't lyin', let's git a closer look.'

The house on their approach, appeared to be in darkness. The ever agile Marco scrambling over a low boundary stone wall, in his excitement, sent a number of stones clattering to the ground. The noise filled Charlie with dread.

'Marco!' he exclaimed, glancing swiftly around, 'us ain't allowed in the grounds.'

'Stop panickin' Charlie, 'ose to know, it's so dark, no-one will see. Follow me.'

'But ... did 'e 'ear that?' Eyes widening, Charlie frozen to the spot, gaped. 'Someones screamin'.'

Inside the darkened grounds, they stood riveted, as a scream broke out from the direction of the house, then another followed by a prolonged eerie silence.

'A woman,' Marco whispered, for no apparent reason. 'There's a light on see ...' Grabbing Charlie's arm, he pointed to the side of the house.

Charlie released his arm, parting and peeping through the shrubbery, he saw a lighted window. A beam from the window lit up the back steps picking out a shadowy form, but what? He screwed up his eyes to get a clearer image.

'A dog, wot's 'e doin' there. Can 'e see it?' asked Marco, turning to Charlie.

'Oscar, the Colonel's dog, 'e's lyin' on the steps?' A puzzled Charlie took another look. 'Somethin's wrong, but wot?' Is 'e dead, a woman's screamin' and the Colonel 'ain't 'round.'

'Dunno, let's find out.' Marco once again, gripped Charlie's arm.

'No ... no!' Charlie, ashen faced and horror-stricken, tried to free it. 'We can't ... us 'ain't allowed!'

'Chicken.' Marco's dark eyes mocked, he smirked.

'I ain't!'

'e is.' The gypsy boy was in no mood for Charlie's excuses.

Not wanting to lose face, dogged by fear with every step, Charlie followed in his footsteps. His heart beating wildly, his eyes fixed on Marco's retreating figure, on hearing the sound of an engine, he dodged behind a thicket. The engine at first spluttering, roared into life, through the gates outside in the lane, he spied a vehicle being driven speedily past. Charlie couldn't believe his eyes, the silvery glow of a full moon emerging from behind a cloud, picked out a green van. He gasped. No it couldn't be, it was. He swung around. But where was Marco? …

CHAPTER 4

W ell,' said Inspector Routley. 'It appears that the Colonel was hit over the head with a blunt instrument, time of death, according to the pathologist, approximately 1 p.m. Do you know of anyone who could have held a grudge against him, that is in the village?'

'Do sit down Inspector, and the Constable too,' said Mrs. Symons, 'how very remiss of me, you'll find the Colonel's chair very comfortable. She patted the seat. 'To think he was only sitting there yesterday.' Her eyes mirrored a sense of loss, she wiped away a tear. 'I can't believe this has happened and to him of all people.'

There, there try and compose yourself, my dear,' said the Inspector, feeling a modicum of pity for the elderly housekeeper, 'but we do have to ask questions.'

'I know, I'm sorry.' Mrs. Symons crossing the room, with a sigh, flopped down on a ornate chair by the leaded window. For a moment silent, she then said, 'Now what was it you wanted?' She rose awkwardly, 'Please excuse me while I open the casement. I need some air … the shock you know.' Cool breezes ruffled the heavy brocade curtains as silently with one work-worn hand on the sill, a frail old lady, she stood looking out onto a garden bathed in morning sunlight.

The Inspector smiled. 'Take your time, Mrs. Symons, we don't mind waiting. Perhaps, a cup of tea?'

'Sugar Inspector?' she asked pouring out his tea on her return, 'One lump or two and perhaps a biscuit, and the constable?'

'To come back to what I was saying.' The Inspector sipped the tea appreciatively. 'Do you know of anyone who could have borne a grudge against him that is from the village or even further afield?'

Cradling a porcelain teacup in her hands, Mrs. Symons for a while, sat deep in thought. 'No I can't think of anybody,' she said, shaking her head, 'that is unless one includes the gypsies. The Colonel you know, kept himself to himself.' Sadly, she shook her head. 'With hardly a word to say to anyone but voiced an opinion about the gypsies if such an occasion arose. It's common knowledge that they are not wanted around here.'

'The gypsies?' The Inspector, puzzled by her remark, raised an eyebrow, for the benefit of a subdued constable scribbling on a notepad.

'Yes an encampment some distance from the village, in Farmer Brown's field.'

'I see, I'll get my constable to make further enquiries. The Inspector relatively pleased when thinking of a possible break through, then asked. 'Are you sure the Colonel didn't have any other worries?'

'He has been depressed since the death of his wife in a car accident.' As if troubled by the effort, the housekeeper gripping the side of the chair for support, heaved herself up. She grimaced, as placing the empty cups back on a silver tray. 'If you ask me, he has never been the same again, not the same man,' her face took on a pained expression.

'Thank you for your time, Mrs. Symons and for the tea.' The Inspector got up. He nodded to the constable. 'At this stage, it appears to be a random robbery from maybe outside the village. Before I go may I?'

'Yes Inspector?'

'Do you know anyone who owns a green van?'

'Why, yes … George, that is, Mr George McDonald, the proprietor of the Nettlebridge General Stores.' Her eyes widened. 'You don't think that he's got anything to do with it, do you?'

෴

CHAPTER 5

But Ma, us 'eard a woman screamin', I'm not lyin'.' Charlie, hanging his head sheepishly, fingered the tassels of his pyjama trousers. After last night, he knew there was no hope in reasoning with her. Anyway, why had Marco left him on his own? Where had he vanished like he did, so quickly into the night? Now the gypsy seemed almost a figment of his imagination, an imaginary friend. By himself he had made his way home where Ma, as he had expected, had been waiting up for him.

Due to the lateness of the hour he had been sent to bed with the promise of a talking to in the morning. Needless to say he hadn't slept, but had lain awake, his mind in torment, gazing vacantly up at shadowy images caste by the moon's glow on the low-beamed ceiling and the trap door to the loft. Exhausted, he had drifted off into a troubled sleep, rudely awakened at cockcrow with bright sunlight streaming in the cottage window, and with the dawn, the inevitable questions.

'Charlie, I'm talking to you, at least have the decency to listen to me, I asked you who you were with?' Ma was not to be trifled with.

'Marco,' he replied, with a lump in his throat, still fingering the tassels.

'Stop fidgeting Charlie, look at me when I'm talking to you. Marco? …' She frowned. 'I don't know any Marco. What a strange name.' As she searched her memory, a thought occurred, prompting her to exclaim, 'Charlie, it's not one of those travellers! She glared at him. 'Well is it?'

Charlie cringed. 'Yes … yes,' he stuttered, wishing he could escape.

'I might have guessed.' She raised her voice.

He backed away.

'I should have known, you couldn't be trusted out of my sight and now with a gypsy boy!' She stormed. 'No doubt he's put wild ideas into your head and on the first day of the summer holidays too!'

Ma was getting more and more exasperated and knowing well from bitter experience the lash of her tongue, Charlie was beginning to wish the floor would swallow him up.

After a while, she calmed down and after a subdued silence, started to put on her hat and coat.

'Where's 'e goin'?' he asked tentatively.

'To the shop.' She firmed her lips. 'Go to your room and stay there 'til your father comes home. Perhaps he'll knock some sense into you.'

'But Ma …' Charlie exclaimed, pulling at her sleeve, 'don' 'e go!'

'Of course, I'm going … let go of me.' She shook herself free. 'Whatever's got into you, control yourself!'

At that moment there was a loud rap at the door. For a second, puzzled, neither spoke but just look at each other. Whoever's that? Ma mouthed.

Oh no, she thought, on opening the door to find a police officer standing on the step. Whatever does he want? So little happened in the village to warrant such a visit.

'Don't tell me, my husband has he been involved in a serious accident.' She gasped at the thought.

The officer, probably from the nearby town, smiled disarmingly and shook his head. Behind him stood Robbie Phillips, Nettleford's own police constable, looking uneasy and slightly out of his depth.

'Inspector Routley from Chillingford Police Constabulary.' He held out an identity card.

So that's where he'd come from, she thought, Chillingford a market town some distance from the village, where if the whim took her she travelled to by train, especially on market days.

'I realise I've no need to introduce the constable as you probably know him. He's standing in for my sergeant whose indisposed.'

Roger blushed. New to the Force, so quite a raw recruit, the sandy haired fresh faced, likeable young constable had been seen on foot or cycling down the street on many occasion. In no time, since his arrival in the village with his vivacious wife, Melanie, he had settled down in the Police House on the edge of the village. A keen gardener, with ornamental shrubs and rockeries, he had transformed an overgrown garden.

In comparison, the Inspector, a stocky built man showed little emotion, his grey eyes practised in the art of observation, automatically taking in the immediate surroundings and its occupants.

Flustered by such an unexpected intrusion into her otherwise routine existence, Iris in an attempt to pull herself together said. 'You'd better come in, I was on my way to the shop, but if I can help in anyway.' She motioned them to sit down.

'To get to the point …' The Inspector paused, he took of his hat, revealing a crop of thick wiry grey hair.

'Can I take it?' asked Iris.

'The hat? No it's alright. As I was saying …'

'Before we start, perhaps, a cup of tea or coffee. Charlie put the kettle on.' At first rendered dumbstruck, in awe of the Inspector, Charlie mumbled, 'But Ma 'e said I wos to go to me room.'

'Not now, put the kettle on and lay out the cups and saucers, make yourself useful,' she said firmly, with one of her 'you do as I say looks.' 'Mind what you're doing you nearly dropped that cup! What's the matter with you, why are you shaking?'

'It must be quite upsetting for the lad.' The kettle boiled, the Inspector taking the proffered cup, felt a twinge of pity.

'I hope Charlie hasn't been up to any mischief. Has that Mildred Marsh been complaining again? She's a dreadful woman? Charlie what have you been doing, your Dad will take a strap to you, you'll be grounded.'

'Nothin' I told you nothin'.'

'May I proceed.' The Inspector drained his cup. 'We are making house to house enquiries about an incident which occurred late last night at the Gables. The constable informs me that shortly after he and his missus had retired for the night, there was a hammering at the door …' He paused. 'You carry on constable.'

'Yes sir' Roger getting up, placed a half empty cup in it's saucer on the table.

'There's no need to stand,' said the Superintendent. 'Carry on.'

Seated, Roger coughed, cleared his throat and began. 'My missus and I had just gone to bed when at approximately 23.00 hours there was a hammering on the door. I picked up my truncheon just in case and opened it. There was a gypsy boy standing on the steps. Distressed and quite out of breath, it was as if he'd been running quite a distance. Panic-stricken, he gabbled incoherently and appeared to be verging on flight. But when lucid, I distinctly heard him say, 'To tell you Mister Policeman …a murder at the big 'ouse.' I tried to calm him down but he slipped free of my grasp, uttering as he fled, 'Me and Charlie, heard it.' A prank, I thought. But the boy would have been a good actor to put on such a performance. And due to severity of the alleged crime, I thought I should investigate.'

'Thank you constable, I'll take over now. Mrs. Blackmore, Mrs Iris Blackmore?'

Iris nodded.

'May I ask you to give an account of your movements and those of your husband between the hours of …'

Iris fixing Charlie with a quizzical look, commented 'So you weren't lying.'

Annoyed by this diversion and her subsequent lack of concentration, the Inspector commented, 'Mrs Blackmore, we were hoping that you would help us with our enquiries.'

'Of course.' Iris drew a deep breath and pursed her lips. 'But there's not much to say. It was just the same as any other day.' She hesitated. 'That is but for Charlie playing truant and staying out all hours.'

He turned to Charlie. 'And your movements, Son?'

'I 'ain't done anythin'.' Charlie's colour rose. 'If that's wot 'e bin thinkin.'

'Sit down lad, and take a deep breath. Just tell me what you remember.'

Iris drew out a kitchen chair. Charlie sat down, his eyes at first downcast. 'I wos wi' Marco.'

'Marco?'

''e's me friend, least I thought 'e wos.'

'And …' prompted the Inspector.

'We wos in the woods. It wos gettin' dark. 'e wos showin' off, 'e said I wos a slowcoach. I got annoyed. I said, if 'e wait, I'll show 'e where the Colonel lives.'

At that moment the telephone shrilled.

'It's for you.' Iris handed the Inspector the receiver.

'Routley here, what now, I'm in the middle of an investigation. Alright if I must, I'll be with you as soon as I can.'

Iris stood by the windowsill. She lifted the net curtains and peered out. The Inspector and Roger engrossed in conversation made their way up the path to the gate, with a click of the latch they were gone. Somewhat mystified and intrigued, she turned away.

'Now what was that all about?' she muttered absentmindedly, her thoughts far away. 'Whatever Charlie had done and it must be Charlie, it couldn't have been anything serious.'

Ma, were 'e talkin' to me?' Startled at the sound of Charlie's voice, she swung around.

Ashen faced, with a pitiful expression, he still stood by the table where the Inspector had left him.

'You were so quiet,' she said, saddened at the sight. 'I quite forgot you were there, what's the matter?'

Sombre eyes in a tearstained face met hers. 'Nothin.' Charlie fumbled in his pyjama pocket, searching for an handkerchief.

'Here take mine,' Iris said in a subdued manner. 'Better still,' she beckoned, 'Come here.'

Charlie stole a glance. 'Wot?'

'I'll wipe it for you.'

'No …No … Leave me alone!' Charlie exclaimed, not wishing to feel more humiliated. Reluctantly, he took the proffered handkerchief and blew his nose noisily.

Perturbed by an apparent breakdown of communication which to her set alarm bells ringing, Iris persisted. 'Charlie what's wrong, you can tell me.'

'I've don' nothin.' He toyed with the soggy handkerchief. 'Can I go to me room?'

'Not now, surely you're not going to sulk.' She sighed, if only Harry was here for what it was worth, to back her up. 'Whatever I suggest, it's only for your own good, you know that.' She held out her hand.

Charlie didn't respond.

'I mean it, I'm listening.' She moved closer to him. 'But don't take long, for I have to go to the shop.'

'Don' 'e leave me 'ere alone!' Charlie moved towards the door in an attempt to block her way.

'But why?' Iris frowned. 'I have to do the shopping.'

She stepped forward and pushed him aside. Dejected, Charlie slumped into a chair near the door, and buried his head in his hands.

It wasn't like Charlie to be so emphatic. Armed with this thought, Iris started to probe.

'What is it?' she pleaded. She knelt in front of him. 'That you can't tell your mother?'

'It's just … just, wot the copper said t'was …' Charlie raised his head and their eyes met.

'What did he say?' Her eyes searched his face for clues. 'Well …'

'It's true Ma, I wos there.'

'What!'

'Wi Marco, us 'eard the woman screamin.'

'The gypsy boy!' Iris's eyes narrowed. 'I might have guessed.' Her voice hardened. 'I told you not to go near their encampment. But what's that got to do with my going to the shop?' Puzzled, she frowned.

'Ma, there wos a green van outside in the lane, I saw it.' He clutched hold of her arm. 'It wos Mr. McDonalds.'

Iris freed herself from his grip. 'Are you sure?'

Charlie nodded.

'Did he drive off in it?'

'T'was dark. I think it wos 'm.' Shoulders hunched, head bent, eyes unfocused, Charlie stared at the floor uncomprehendingly. ''e wos in a 'urry.'

Iris got up. 'It couldn't have been George,' she cried, 'he wouldn't have been out at that time of night delivering goods, would he?'

'e must 'ave bin.' Charlie uncomfortable and ill at ease, saw her remark as a means to end a rather tiresome conversation.

'Must have been what?' Iris gazed into the hallstand mirror and straightened her hat at a rakish angle.

'Makin' a delivery, a late one.' Charlie rose. 'Is that all Ma?'

'No that's not all.' Iris's steely blue eyes flashed, her tone registered disapproval. 'If you're making up stories ...'

'No Ma, Scout's 'onour!'

'If that's so why didn't you tell the Inspector what you've told me, not half a story.'

'cause I'm 'fraid ... Charlie's voice faltered. 'Fraid that 'e would think that ...

'You were involved, weren't you?' Iris's tone of voice, generated fear.

'No! Can I go?' Charlie stepped towards the door.

Exasperated Iris sighed. 'And that gypsy boy, Marco. Is that his name? You're not to see him again.' She picked up her wicker shopping basket and leather handbag. 'I won't be long. You'll be safe here, I'll lock the door, behind me. Now go to your room and stay there until your father comes home. At least I'll know where to find you.' The front door clicked shut behind her, Charlie heard the key turn in the lock.

So that's it, back to square one, Charlie thought. He wearily made his way up stairs. Laying stretched out on his bed, his arms behind his head, he muttered, 'So Marco's bin to the Police 'Ouse, without tellin' me, some friend 'e is.'

❧

Iris stood on the doorstep and checked her shopping list. No there wasn't anything she had forgotten. She looked up at the sky. With no sign of the sun, it was cloudy and overcast, but with no wind, little chance of rain. Pity, she thought, for the gardens were parched.

Tomorrow being Sunday, she had set her heart on a nice leg of lamb, she had spotted in the butchers shop window. Amos

Higgins, a chirpy little man, with a ready smile and a handle-bar moustache, would have set it aside, if she'd had the presence of mind to ask him in passing. Hopefully, it was still there. She pictured it, succulent, roasted to a turn, smothered in lashings of gravy, with mint sauce, crispy potatoes, garden peas and home grown carrots. Her appetite wetted, she licked her lips. As to a dessert, she didn't mind, whatever Harry and the boy wanted, it would be a change.

Iris quickened her pace, for to her there weren't enough hours in the day. Gone were all thoughts of the Inspector's visit, which she had dismissed as just one of those things, for he had left so abruptly.

Someway ahead she caught sight of Emily coming in her direction. The old lady made slow progress. She carried a shopping bag with apparently not much in it, agitated, she fingered a scrap of paper.

Intrigued, drawing abreast, Iris heard her mutter. 'Fancy, without warning. You'd think he ...'

'What Emily, what warning?'

Startled Emily looked up, her faded blue eyes at first unfocused, soon got their bearings. 'Oh it's you Iris, how nice.' She mustered up a smile.

'What warning, Emily?' Iris persisted.

'The shops closed and I ...' Emily frowned, 'I wanted some potatoes amongst other things for tomorrow.'

'Wasn't there a notice on the door, some explanation?' Iris felt a jerk reaction, an inexplicable sinking feeling that something must have gone terribly wrong.

'I couldn't see anything, still my eyesight not so good as it was. And I couldn't find my spectacles. Now, where did I put them?' Emily rummaged in her bag. 'Ah, there they are!' She glanced back at the shop. 'But what am I going to do now?' She said in a small voice.

'Good morning, ladies. It's clouding over still ...'

Neither Emily nor Iris had been aware of the Reverend Ralph Watson's rapid approach on his bicycle. With a squeal of brakes, he skidded to a halt and stopped in front of them. Emily jumped, her already fragile nerves, shattered.

'So sorry, I must get some oil before trying the bike out again.' The Vicar patted Emily's thin shoulders. 'Perhaps a new machine.'

'So you don't know.' Iris brushed aside his remark as irrelevant. 'The village store is closed, with not so much as a by your leave, I would have thought George would been more considerate.'

'I'm sorry ladies,' the Vicar propping his bike against a wall, blew his nose. 'I don't know what to say, perhaps George is ill or there's an illness in the family. Are they in easy reach?'

'I wouldn't know,' said Iris, 'he doesn't talk about his private life, I always thought he was a bachelor.'

'I'll make some enquiries, leave it to me. That's the least I can do. We can't have Emily going without her groceries, can we?' Ralph's face crumbled into a smile. 'You never know, in time George with a little persuasion, may even attend Sunday Services, let's hope so.'

Iris glanced at her wrist watch. 'What a nuisance.' She sighed. I shall have to ask Harry to run me into Chillingford when he comes home from the saw mill.'

'You wouldn't, you couldn't,' stammered Emily, blushing with embarrassment.

'Of course, Iris replied sympathetically, 'we'll pick you up, shall we say six o'clock.'

With a sense of pity, Iris stood alongside the Vicar and watched the frail old lady, clutching her bag, make her way homewards past the church gates, until she vanished from sight.

'Poor soul,' she murmured. 'It must be awful to get old.'

'We'll all get old one day.' The Vicar sneezed. 'Hay fever,' he said in response to Iris's raised eyebrow. I'm a prey to it this time of year.' He mounted his bike, 'I must be off. Back to the vicarage, there's a sermon I need to rewrite. See you tomorrow in church hopefully.'

As she made her way homeward, Iris conjectured. Suppose Charlie was right, maybe George was involved. What exactly had happened at the Gables? So many questions unanswered. So far she hadn't met anyone who knew, how could she have when no-one seemed to be around. Someone, somewhere must know something surely. George may not have been driving the van. Charlie didn't seem to know for certain. But, even if he had been, there might have been a rational explanation, for after all George wouldn't stoop to any skulduggery, or would he?

❧

CHAPTER 6

The evening was drawing to a close, in another hour, the sun, a hazy sphere would dip below the rounded hills and dense woodlands. At present, the warmth of it's rays lingered, although not in the cool interior of the church, there shadowy images merged in dim recesses where in light relief, stain glass windows shed myriad coloured beams of light.

With an echo of footsteps, Mildred Marsh alone with her dark thoughts, paced the flagstone floors, to her every creak, every rustle, a threat, the oaken church door ajar, the silence broken only with the muted sounds of a dying day. Once more she envisaged the fearful, uncomprehending look in the Colonel's eyes, a mirror image of what she herself had felt in the cold light of day. What had possessed her? Her contempt of the gypsies? She vaguely remembered stepping over the bloodied body of the dog, outside the kitchen door. She had paused briefly on the bottom step. Was the old man dead or still breathing? He had gone a deathly white. Panic-stricken, bleary eyed, searching for George and the green van, she had run at random, away from the awful scene.

Her back aching, Mildred lowered herself onto the altar steps, her grey eyes reflecting the pain. She stretched out her legs. Her stockings were torn. Cuts, bruises and congealed blood, brought back a vague recollection of a wild scramble over high bricked walls, across muddy ditches, through neighbouring farmer's fields, the word 'sanctuary' forever ringing in her ears.

Where was George? Should they have used the Master Plan? To disguise themselves as gypsies for the final haul? And what of the loot stacked in the loft at the cottage? She had banked on George's help, to shift and dispose of it with a series of journeys in the green van to an unknown destination. Now not knowing his whereabouts, anything could happen.

The worst scenario, if he cracked under the strain and talked, she would deny all knowledge, implying a nervous breakdown. He had been very wound up about his shop at times. Who could fail to believe her? Although not liked, she still regarded herself as a pillar of the community. Still how to dispose of the loot without any transport or help. She would think things out. Take the train and visit her sister? She hadn't seen her for years. Leave the booty behind to pick up on her return, when things died down? Make up a sob story?

She glanced at her watch and started to rearrange the altar flowers, a creature of habit, she had missed her turn. But what about her stockings? In the vestry she peeled them off, and doused her legs with water. Next, laid out the cassocks, freshly laundered, on the little table by the window, in readiness for the Sunday Service. But wasn't prepared for what would happen next.

She had just disposed of her stockings in the waste bin, when the church door creaked open. 'Who can it be at this hour?' she murmured. Her heart thumping, ears pricked, she held her breath, and listened intently. There it was again, a movement, footsteps, then silence. She took a deep breath. 'Don't be silly!' She admonished herself. 'It can only be the Vicar.' She glanced at her legs. 'Even so, no stockings! What will he think?' She patted her hair and peeped around the vestry door.

In the dim light, the outline of a male figure was framed against the open doorway. A bulky one not like the Vicars. But whose? Her mouth felt dry. Someone must be looking for her. George must have panicked and given them away. But how would he have known, she was here? She glanced desperately around. There would be nowhere to hide. She gasped. But, what if it was an intruder or even an assassin. She fingered the cross on the chain she wore around her neck, and voiced a whispered prayer. 'Spare me O Lord.'

'Pull yourself together!' Again, she admonished herself. 'It can only be the Vicar. Yes, that's who it is.' She gave herself a mental pat on the back.

She stepped out of the vestry. 'Is that you Ralph, it's only me. I suppose …' She stopped in mid-sentence, as the figure moved.

'Missus.'

The sound of the rough voice grated. Who could it be, surely not one of the villagers? The man had the deep phlegmy voice of a heavy smoker. She wrinkled her nose in disgust.

'Yes?' she said abruptly. She put on her glasses to get a closer look.

'Where's the station, the Police 'ouse that is ?'

The man's voice, gruff, hesitant but persistent, set her thinking.

'Who can it be?' she muttered, searching her mind. 'There was something familiar, the mannerisms, but what?' She froze, when conjuring up a picture of an undesirable image.

'Oh no!' She gasped. 'Not one of them, and here of all places!' Was it the traveller she had seen in the village or another one? They all looked the same and filled her with disgust, for weren't they unwashed, uneducated, and irresponsible.

With a face like thunder, she stomped down the aisle. 'Get out!' She cried as coming face to face with him. 'You're not wanted here.'

The gypsy stood his ground. 'T'is important Missus, I must get to the station, the Police 'ouse that is. My names Mario, Marco's Pa. T'is 'bout that gent, the Colonel. Our Marco told me.' He stopped abruptly on seeing Mildred's unrelenting stony expression.

'Why?' she sneered, 'Are you going to give yourself up, about time too?'

A proud man, Mario chose to ignore her comment, only too aware from past experiences, of the unjustified reputation of the gypsies. He knew he had nothing to hide. He eyed her for a moment.

His dark eyes mesmerised her, unable to meet his scrutiny, Mildred turned away, heeding the dictates of her subconscious, fearful, of showing any weakness.

'Our Marco saw somethin' that night.' He cleared his nasal passages noisily, a contemptuous sound, which filled her with dread. 'A green van driven way at speed up a lane. 'e 'eard a woman screamin' from the big 'ouse.'

Mildred heart sank. She plucked up her courage, and with a disdainful look retorted, 'Whose going to believe you, a gypsy. I wouldn't be surprised if you were all involved.' Her eyes glinted. 'Well, weren't you?'

Mario's expression and indifference, infuriated her even more. Her head and back ached so badly it was hard to focus on him. Forgetting all precedence in such hallowed surroundings, she muttered. 'Who does he think he is, I'll show him!'

A red mist descending, embodied her, with a sudden movement, with a crazed look, as that of a predatory animal, she sprung, in an attempt to grab his arm.

He stepped back.

'No you don't, I haven't finished with you yet!' She cried, her body unflinching, her voice raised in anger. 'You can go when I say or not at all, do you hear me?'

The Vicar clutching the rewritten sermon he had taken such pains over earlier that afternoon, about to turn the corner, intimidated by the noise, kept out of sight. Something held him back. Was it divine providence or merely a premonition? Whatever it was, he stood riveted to the spot.

෴

CHAPTER 7

With a peal of church bells, the sun broke through thin layers of whitish-grey cloud cover. 'Where's Charlie?' Iris asked herself aloud. She stood and studied her reflection in the hallstand mirror, yet again adjusting her new hat at a rakish angle. It sat perfectly on her raven black hair, under it's brim, violet blue eyes appraised her. Not so bad for my age, better than some, they seem to say. Here and there a grey hair, maybe lines on her forehead and the suggestion of a frown mark, but otherwise pretty good.

'What another hat!' Harry exclaimed. 'Frittering away my hard-earned lolly.' He gave it a cursory glance, but carried along with her enthusiasm, remarked with a ghost of a smile, 'But you look nice.'

The cream wide brimmed hat, dressed with a spray of summer roses, complimented a navy blue and cream two piece, and matching accessories. She felt a million dollars. She twirled to get a last full-length look.

It promised another hot day, tempered by a light breeze. Iris finding the kitchen oppressively hot, pushed open the back door. Standing on the step, she fanned herself with a rolled up newspaper. Outside in the bricked backyard, she caught sight of Harry tinkering under the bonnet of their old Morris Minor.

'Where's Charlie?' She cried, her voice carried.

Harry put down an oily spanner, mopped his brow with his shirt sleeve and looked up. He frowned. 'Isn't he in his bedroom?

'I'll see and you better change, we'll be leaving for Church in ten minutes.'

The staircase creaked, Iris swung around.

A solemn faced Charlie stood on the bottom step.

'And where do you think you're going, creeping around like a alley cat, you frightened the daylights out of me!' she exclaimed.

'Nowhere Ma,' Charlie replied sheepishly.

'You're coming to Church with your father and I.' She eyed him suspiciously. 'Do you understand?'

'ave I got to?' Charlie's face fell. 'It's borin' …' His voice tailed off.

Iris sighed. 'We have to keep up appearances, don't we.'

Charlie in a gloomy frame of mind, dawdled.

On their approach, from the church porch, Iris heard the subdued murmur of the congregation from within. She drew in her breath. 'I just knew we'd be late.' She grimaced. 'You should set an example to the boy, Harry.'

'I was ready.' Harry shrugged his shoulders. 'You can take a horse to water but you can't make it drink, can you?'

'Really.' Iris commented derisively. She turned and caught sight of a disgruntled Charlie lagging behind. 'Come on,' she called, 'hurry up.'

Inside, mellowed by the strains of organ music, Iris having discreetly caste an eye, patted the side of the pew, an indication to Charlie as to where he should sit. Reluctantly, he sat down beside his mother, his eyes fixed on his highly polished shoes.

Half way through the service, Iris nudged Harry, whispering in his ear, 'Money for the collection.'

She watched the church warden take the bag from pew to pew and in so doing noticed Mildred Marsh was no-where to be seen. 'I wonder where she is,' she muttered. 'She never misses a service.'

They sang several hymns, had a bible reading, before the Vicar stood up to give the address. He seemed detached, his face pallid and drawn, as if he hadn't slept.

Is his wife ill? Iris wondered, or his daughter? Neither were present.

Perhaps the Vicar's mood reflected the vicious and unprovoked attack on the Colonel at 'The Gables,' and the old man's subsequent coma. 'Thou shalt not steal' 'The perpetrators of the crime,' he said, 'had thought otherwise. No good had come out of it, now they were on the run. In one of our flock's darkest hours, let us offer up our prayers for a full recovery.'

Outside in the fresh air, Harry sensed Iris was withdrawn. He tapped her on the back. 'Come on, let's go for a walk, it'll cheer you up.'

'Not me too? Charlie, who had been wandering about in the churchyard, kicked a stone down the road.

'Yes! You too!' Harry firmed his lips. 'And don't lag behind this time.'

'And don't scuff your new shoes.' Iris cried, a scornful look in her eyes.

∽∾∿

CHAPTER 8

George MacDonald slowed down, pulled onto a grassy verge, and switched off the ignition. It was a lonely stretch of road; but after the turmoil of the past few hours, he was glad to find solace in such tranquil surroundings. He unfastened his seat belt, half opened the window, then leant back in his seat and closed his eyes. He would take a well earned nap. At least, that is what he thought. He hadn't bargained for an active mind, filled with uncertainties.

Why had he come back to the village after so many years? He'd often wondered. Was it to see his son, now a schoolboy on a daily basis? He had a right to, hadn't he? After all, the boy was his own flesh and blood. Or was it to see Iris? What did he hope to gain? The only woman he truly loved and would have married had found happiness with another man. Iris face to face, with loss of memory now saw him now merely as the village storekeeper. Even so, as if to torment himself, he had stayed fixed to the spot, lavishing all his care and attention on the shop, as he would have on her, but what for? Had the past come back to haunt him?

Then Mildred Marsh came on the scene. He had taken an instant dislike to her. Her gossiping was more than the average person could digest, and that included George. Standing behind the counter, he had listened at length to her character assassination of the gypsies. They weren't popular, it was true, but neither were they responsible for all the village's anti-social behaviour. The thought that he would become the next victim of Mildred's venom, hadn't occurred.

One afternoon she confronted him with a yellowing newspaper cutting. He gasped. He denied all knowledge of the scandal. But, he was no match for her. Should he inform the police? No, the scandal would have been too much for him to bear.

Mildred Marsh was cunning, bringing to the fore an event long buried in the past.

Perhaps I should model myself on the Colonel, live in isolation; buy a dog, a home-help once a week, George thought. One morning, he remarked to the Colonel's housekeeper, 'As I see it, the Colonel is prey to vagabonds and thieves.' Little did he know that he would be one of them. Everyone knew that the Mrs. Symons only slept in at weekends, leaving the Old Boy alone in that big house from Monday to Friday. This would be Mildred Marsh's trump card.

When Mildred first revealed her plan to rob the Colonel, George had dismissed it as wishful thinking. She wouldn't dare carry it out, would she? But he was wrong, she had threatened him, George with exposure, if he didn't back her plan.

Fearful he had acquiesced, with not one but many more raids, the Colonel failing in health, none the wiser. But, their time was running out.

That final evening at dusk, George had parked his van just before the gates. Mildred tumbled out of the front passenger seat. George followed. Stealthily they approached the wide wrought iron gates. Through the ornate bars lay an expanse of manicured grass, behind which stood the formidable outline of 'The Gables,' with no lights from the leaden windows, the house in darkness.

'We've timed it well.' George heard Mildred's muffled voice. 'The Old Boy's retired for the night. Stay on my heels,' she whispered in George's ear. She shot back the bolt. Hardly daring to breath, George followed her through the gates. The crunch of the grit underfoot jarred. Every shadow took on a human form, an owl hooted.

'My God!' he hissed.

They neared the house.

'What's that?' She froze.

George jerked his head. 'Where?'

Mildred screwed up her hawk-like eyes, homed them on the shrubbery.

The inky darkness kept its secrets.

George tapped Mildred's shoulder. 'Somebody's watching.'

'Get a grip, Man'. She growled.

An upstairs light pierced the shadows. Without speaking, they dropped to the ground.

The toilet flushed. Darkness reigned, again

They got to their feet. George flicked off gravel embedded in his palms.

Mildred gave thought to her Grand Plan, and its declared aim to rob the Colonel. So far, everything had gone to plan. The key for the kitchen door, under a plant pot, having no sooner inserted it in the lock, she had unwittingly knocked over a galvanised bucket.

On hearing an unfamiliar sound, Oscar, the golden retriever woke up suddenly. He growled, and without warning leapt at Mildred. She sensed danger, felt blood surging through her pulse. Grabbing a wooden rolling pin from a work surface she sprang into action. She lashed out, her face contorted with rage, she screamed. 'Help me finish him off.'

Petrified, George stood on the threshold and watched. This was the first time he had seen brute force used against a domestic animal by a woman, or a man. Was this the same woman who had smiled so innocently in church? Violence wasn't on the agenda. Should he warn the Colonel?

A voice boomed in the passageway, 'What the blazes?' With a shuffling of slippers and the flick of a light switch, a form emerged. The Colonel was framed in the doorway.

'Mildred … it's you.' His questioning eyes met her cold calculating stare. 'What are you doing?' He glanced at the empty dog basket, the bloodstains on the tiled floor. 'Oscar … what's happened to him?'

He stumbled towards the half open kitchen door.

'Oh no, you don't.' Arms akimbo, Mildred barred his way.

'But I must … Oscar! Oscar! Where are you? The Colonel's rheumy eyes fixed on the doorway. He made a feeble attempt to push her aside, but her demons couldn't be assuaged.

Mildred lunged at the frail old man.

'Stop! ... Stop it,' screamed George. 'You'll kill him.' The words stuck in his throat. The police? he thought, Call the police, but if he spoke to them, he would incriminate himself. Spend a few years inside. His mind in a quandary, he watched Mildred with the rolling pin, batter the defenceless old man.

Whimpering, the dog itself, lay on the steps, bleeding profusely from numerous wheals on its body. George, traumatised by the sight, the old man's desperate cries ringing in his ears, ran blindly, down the gravel drive, and out onto the lane. He jumped into his van, turned the ignition key. The engine groaned. A sense of panic seized him 'Oh God not now!' As if in answer to his unspoken prayer, it coughed., and he had roared off, far, far away to the ends of the earth if he had had his way. Far away from pointing fingers, from Mildred's hostility, from the sight of her thin lips, lips that would turn the tables, that would reveal all.

He envisaged a mental picture of his mother, divorced and embittered, at odds with the world, always attempting to control his life. Strangely enough, her attitude not unlike Mildred's, as Mildred's with time becoming demanding. He'd never forget that day of days when he'd told her, about the accident, hoping against hope for some support and advice but finding none.

If only he hadn't taken his eyes off the road for one split second that day, when Iris had told him that she was pregnant. Then thinking what he knew his mother would say, as she had so many times before. 'You've been with that hussy, she'll be the ruin of you. You listen to me, or you'll rue the day.'

He had listened and had rued the day. After making Iris comfortable, convinced that she would soon be found, he had left her lying unconscious by the wayside. She had been, but with a loss of memory never regained and a subsequent premature birth. From that moment, it was if a veil had descended upon her, as if their relationship had never existed.

He had had problems at first in tracking down Iris, and hadn't even known the gender of the child, but had at last found out from an acquaintance at his mother's funeral where she was. She hadn't changed a bit and was as beautiful as ever.

He found no solace when thinking that she had no recollection of him since that fateful day, when seeing her in the shop and walking down the village street on a regular basis. He had willed himself to accept the situation for the need to see the boy in close proximity or even at a distance was paramount.

Consequently, with his help, the Colonel's valuable antiques and object d'art much to his consternation were gradually becoming depleted. Mildred's intention was only to use the Master Plan when any suspicion of their loss was addressed. To disguise as gypsies with a final raid, they would make their getaway, leave the village behind for good. It beggared belief why the Colonel or his elderly housekeeper hadn't tumbled to what was going on. They proved an easy prey for a pitiless predator.

So carried away was Mildred, that on one occasion, a glint in her eye, she had commented, much to his disgust, 'It will suit you as much as I, won't it?'

One of George's migraines was now coming on. He opened the glove compartment where he habitually kept a bottle of aspirins and sometimes some whisky for medicinal purposes. The bottle was full, and there were plenty of aspirins. A dark thought crossed his mind. Here, he was stranded in the middle of nowhere, he'd messed up his life. What was the point of his existence, no-one would miss him, would they? For a few moments, he studied the amber nectar as unscrewing the cap of the pill bottle. 'Was this really the answer?' he asked himself.

≈

CHAPTER 9

Charlie, behave yourself!

'I 'ain't doin' nothin…' Charlie was beginning to get bored and lagging behind at that moment, was momentarily kicking yet another stone along the lane. Frustrated, his thoughts were with the gypsy encampment, wishing he was there. He bet the gypsies didn't waste needless hours in church. He missed Marco. Where was he now, what was he doing, he wondered and would he ever see him again. No doubt, Ma would put a stop to that.

'I told you not to do that!' Ma's angry voice dispelled these dark thoughts. 'You're scuffing your new shoes and dirtying your clothes with the dust.'

Charlie pulled a face, he knew there was no point in arguing. 'Alright then,' he responded begrudgingly 'where are we goin' anyway?'

'Your father and I thought that it would be nice, if the three of us, took a walk after church.' Iris smiled, her face took on a compromising look. 'It being Sunday?'

'Is that all.' Charlie's current dark mood deepened. 'I thought it may 'ave bin special, bein' dressed up an' all. Can I go 'ome now?'

Harry sympathised, after church, he normally would have been found in the Blue Boar with his mates propping up the bar, but from the moment Iris put on that hat, he might have known something was up. 'What about making our way to the Gables,' he suggested when seeing Charlie's doleful expression. Seeing a spark of interest, he added with a twinkle in his eye, 'It would please your mother seeing she's dressed for the occasion.'

'Would it.' Iris gave Harry a withering look. 'I don't remember giving that impression at all, still why not, it will be somewhere to go.'

For a while they walked in silence, each step, Charlie's enthusiasm waning, with Iris impeding their progress. She fussed constantly about her new outfit and hat, and even declined Harry's suggestion, that she should go home and change. Eventually, much to Charlie's relief, they reached the outskirts of the village where in the distance, could be seen the Gables, it's façade shining in the morning sunlight.

'Here we are at last.' Iris by the main gates, straightened her skirt. From her handbag, she took out a powder compact, scrutinized her face and applied some fresh lipstick.

'Is that necessary,' commented Harry dryly.

'One never knows, who one may meet does one in a place like this?' She replied tartly.

'I should think there's little chance of that, it looks like the gates are padlocked.' Harry peered through the bars at the manicured lawns and sweeping gravel drive.

'I'm not coming all this way, just to go home.' Iris rattled the gates. 'Can't you do anything Harry?'

'I don't see the point.' Harry said, eyeing not one but two padlocks. 'There's bound to be a police presence, although I can't see any.' A worried frown creased his brow. 'I really think we ought to call it a day.'

'Don' 'e go 'ome yet.' Charlie, who until now had not spoken, broke into the conversation. 'I knows 'ow to git in.'

'What sort of way?' Iris looked doubtful.

'Over there, Marco an'I found it.' Charlie led the way through long grasses fringing high boundary walls, on the right hand side of the property.

'So you were here and with that gypsy too, you've got a lot of explaining to do my boy, once I get you home!' Iris exclaimed. Eyeing the crumbling stonework with an air of foreboding, she felt compelled to say, 'If there's any climbing, I might let you know, I've my best clothes on and I don't want to ladder my stockings.' She hesitated. 'Come to think of it, it's private land, we'd be trespassing, and I for one don't want to be arrested.'

Charlie climbing up, scanned the other side of the wall. 'Come on Ma, no-ones 'bout.' He held out a helping hand. 'Don' 'e be a spoil sport.'

'Oh, alright then, since we've come all this way.' By now overcome with curiosity, and much against her better judgement with the help of Harry and Charlie, Iris in a rather undignified manner, clutching her hat, scrambled up. What had possessed her to join in this hare brained scheme? She wondered, on seeing her scratched legs and laddered stockings. 'My, my ... but here's a sight for sore eyes!' She exclaimed, as from a height, scanning an expanse of far reaching lawns. 'I always wondered what the Colonel's place looked like close up.'

Gingerly they picked their way across the grass towards the house, each instinctively drawn to the leaden casements, some boarded up from prying eyes. At the side of the house they came upon an overgrown narrow path.

Iris fearful of an authoritative figure, manifesting itself at any given moment, glancing feverishly around, soon lagged behind.

Charlie and Harry who had been leading the way, stopped for a time beside a water butt just outside the kitchen door, waiting for Iris to catch up. 'Where I is now, Oscar wos lyin,' Charlie bursting to tell her on her approach, indicated the stone steps 'but 'e's gone, I wonder wot 'appened to 'im?'

'The Colonel's dog?' mumbled Iris, her eyes drawn to the window. Unboarded, it's panes were covered in grime. With her handkerchief, she vigorously rubbed the ingrained dirt, in a futile attempt to see inside.

'I shouldn't waste time doing that, Iris', said Harry, 'It's ingrained, and you won't see much.'

For once, Iris had to admit that Harry was right. She turned to Charlie, 'What did you say, Oscar's gone? I shouldn't worry about that, perhaps he was taken away by a vet.'

'Let's go 'round back' Charlie started to wander down the path.

'I don't know, do you think we ought.' Iris caste a cursory glance at Harry.

'I don't know what to say,' Harry gave her a sheepish look. 'You make up your own mind, I don't want to be blamed for talking you into doing the wrong thing.'

'Alright, why not just a peep.' Iris glanced at her watch. 'But we better not be long, it's nearly dinnertime.'

At the rear of the house they came upon a number of outbuildings. In one corner stood a large greenhouse standing in the shelter of an old oak tree, the branches of which swung precariously, in a late morning breeze. Much the worse for wear, with several panes broken, peeling paint and it's door creaking on its hinges; it possessed an air of neglect, in stark contrast to the manicured lawns, so admired by Iris.

Picking their way over the uneven surfaces of a large weatherworn patio, crannies and cracks sprouting a profusion of weeds, they reached the outbuildings. In one they found a collection of gardening implements. Stacked against a whitewashed wall festooned with cobwebs, some were discarded and rusty, others relatively new. Most of the buildings were empty, all but one in which they were to find in one corner, tins of paint, miscellaneous brushes and a heap of old overalls.

'Harry, come out here, whatever's that?' Iris's shrill voice broke the silence.

Harry and Charlie having emerged looked in the direction to which she pointed. Dazzled by the sunlight, shielding their eyes, at first they could see nothing, but their eyes having adjusted, a dark shape moving through the thick undergrowth bordering the pastureland beyond.

'Why it's a feral!' exclaimed Harry.

'I only see a cat,' said Iris, 'Come on let's go over and make friends.' She started to pick her way.

'No … No!' exclaimed Harry. 'Don't touch it, don't go near!'

'Why?' asked Charlie and Iris almost in unison.

'Because it's not like a domestic cat, it's a little tiger, leave it alone!'

'I'm going to take a look anyway,' remarked Iris, stubborn to the core.

''e ain't no tiger.' Charlie was intrigued.

'So alike,' Harry thought, as ruefully, he watched them approach the cat. 'They'll learn.'

The cat crawling out of the undergrowth, padded leisurely in the direction of the greenhouse. It seemed totally unaware of their presence, it's nondescript colour, lean body and sharp eyes indicating it's sole intention. It suddenly stopped and crouched stock still, it's intended victim, an unsuspecting bird, in a flurry of protests, taking to the wing just-in-time, leaving an indignant cat waving it's tail.

'Poor thing, it looks half-starved.' Iris moved closer to get a better look.

Harry shook his head in dismay. 'I told you, leave it alone, it will bite you.'

'Look,' said Charlie. 'e's making its way to the oak tree. e's scavengin' under a pile of dead leaves, wot's 'e found?'

'Whatever it is, it can't be very nice with all those flies. And ugh, what a horrible smell!' Iris with a lace-edged handkerchief covered her nose.

The cat now aware of their presence, stood up and with a fixed look in their direction, let out a strange cry. To Harry's relief, turning tail, it dived into the thick undergrowth.

'Let's see what it was so interested in, however distasteful it may be.' said an ever curious Iris, tossing her head coquettishly in Harry's direction, she smirked. 'I assume I may, with your permission.'

'Ma, don' 'e come any closer!' Charlie was already standing by the pile. 'It stinks, 'tis 'orrible an' …' He clasped his hands over his eyes.

Harry joined him. 'There's no doubt about it, as I thought it would be.' He said, 'It's Oscar.'

'Poor Oscar, whatever could have happened?' Iris feeling quite sick, turned away, when seeing the decomposed body of the dog, they had known and loved. The smell was horrendous and the flies were having a field day, but it didn't deter her from saying, 'We must give him a proper burial, he deserves that.'

'You want me to do it, I suppose,' said Harry, not relishing the prospect.

'Yes' said Iris, 'Charlie, collect some wood and make a make-shift cross, I'll pick some wild flowers and then we'll say a few prayers, after all it is Sunday.'

'Yes Ma-am,' Harry raising his arm in a mock salute, grinned. 'Anything else?'

'Oscar's dead!' Charlie stood by the newly dug grave. 'e didn't deserve that,' he sobbed, tears flowing unashamedly. 'Did 'e?'

෴

CHAPTER 10

The gypsy camp was quiet and deserted, even the dogs were subdued by the heat. Some had found solace lying in the damp grasses fringing the field, others in the shade of a copse.

The wolf hound keeping a watchful eye on a number of piebald horses cropping nearby, had become restless. Happy and content up until now the dog had lain in the shade of a tree, with no desire to wander or investigate.

'Nothin' much 'appening 'round 'yer,' Mario remarked, wiping the perspiration from his forehead with a now very grubby handkerchief. He stood up and glanced around, arms akimbo. 'Not a soul … Salvador must 'ave gone fishin' or else to the pub, that's if 'e can find one wot don' chuck 'im out.' He chuckled. 'And Lorenza, 'e'd be goin' door to door wi' the cart.'

''aven't seen Amica for a bit, 'ave 'e, Mario?' Marco yawned. ''er must 'ave sold them pegs, lets 'ope so.'

'Yea, tis 'bout time Salvador made more. 'e used to be a good basket maker when 'e wundn't hittin' the bottle, weren't 'e?'

Marco was bored. Sitting within earshot on the bank, dangling his feet in the cool waters of the stream, he didn't at first respond, his mind elsewhere, on that of a stick he had just thrown into its sparkling depths. Mesmerised by it's passage downstream, he said 'Talkin' of bottles. If I 'ad a bottle, I'd stuff a message inside some bode might find it.'

'There me 'andsome, that's better 'aint it?' said Mario after shoeing a horse. He patted it's chestnut rump, straining on its tether in the shade of a sycamore tree, it neighed an appreciative response. 'Bottle, wot bottle, Son?'

'Doesn' matter.' By now Marco had lost interest.

'Marco, where's Marco?' A strident female voice resounded across the field. Not far away, Eliza had been washing the family's clothes in the sunlit stream. She cupped her hands over her eyes, scanned the field.

'Marco's over 'ere with me, Mother, wot do 'e want, now?' Mario's gruff voice carried.

A loud wail broke the silence, followed by a cry of desperation, 'Can't 'e look after Juanita, 'ers gettin' under me feet.'

Breathless and bedraggled, Eliza clutching the hand of the petulant child, joined Mario and Marco on the bank. 'Marco, I wos wonderin' …?'

'Marco, I wants Marco.' A little voice persisted.

'Not me agin. I took 'er fer a walk yesterday.' Marco protested, determined not to be intimidated by his little sister, he turned away.

Her little face crumbled. She pouted her lips.

'Give the boy a break, Mother.' Mario felt sorry for his son. ''e's bin helpin' out quite a bit lately, since 'e's stopped seein' that village boy.'

'I 'adn't noticed.' grumbled Eliza. 'And I asks you, when do I 'ave a break, from washin' your dirty clothes?'

Her temper rising, Mario quickly changed the topic. 'Where's the dog?'

'Up in the wagon, the last time I saw 'im. Shall I see if 'e's still there?' Marco grasped the opportunity to free himself of his mother's scrutinising look.

'Good idea, Son,' said Mario, suppressing a sly smile. 'Off 'e go.'

The mottled grey dog sprawled in the shade of the wagon raised his head as Marco approached. He pricked his ears, rose from his haunches, stretched his long legs and shook himself.

'Come on Boy.'

The old dog, saliva dribbling from his muzzle, padded lethargically towards what he thought his Master. Marco patted his head, named Rover, the dog responded by wagging his tail, his brown eyes under straggly tufts of hair, monitoring Marco's every move.

'The dog's fitter,' Eliza smiled. 'I really thought 'e wos a goner.'

Mario sighed. 'Yea, wi im peppered with shots. But wot do us want wi another dog? On the move, plenty will follow.' He ruffled the dog's furry coat. 'On t'other 'and, us gypsies, never turns a dog away, if 'e wants ter stay, who am I to say no?'

'Juanita, wants dog.' A little voice piped up.

'Tiny ears, 'ears wot they shouldn't,' Eliza picked up the little girl. 'The dogs too big fer 'e, Juanita.'

Juanita was not impressed. She stared at the dog, screwed up her little face and started to cry once more, between sobs, yelling, 'I wants it!'

'Stop yer bawlin'girl, look wot I've got.' Eliza held out a rather dilapidated teddy bear. For a moment this diversion pacified the little girl, but not for long. Tearful, she tossed the teddy aside when catching sight of Marco with the dog. Frustrated, Eliza propelling a struggling Juanita towards the wagon, once there, bundled her up the steps and slammed the door.

'Peace at last.' Mario seated on a grassy mound, lit an old clay pipe. With a cursory glance at Marco, he asked, 'Well son, wot wos 'e thinkin' of doin'?'

'Don' know.' Marco looked down at the dog, now laying on his side. 'Can't think of anythin' 'cept a walk.' The dog's ears twitched.

'e 'aven't seen yer mate from the village. Wot's 'e's name?' Mario frowned, scratched his head. 'Albert, Sammy 'er somethin'?'

'It's Charlie. No, I ain't since the night of the robbery. I wun goin' to 'ang around, git on the wrong side of the law. Ma reckons I should stick to the woods, 'unt rabbits or fish, rather than 'ang out wi' village boys.'

Mario mused. 'Tell 'e wot I'm thinkin'.'

'Wot?'

'Why don't us make a day of it, go fishin' downstream. Jest us two an' the dog. Wot do 'e think?'

'Great!' Marco was ecstatic. 'Wot 'bout the water bailiff?'

'Wot 'bout 'im? The fish will taste tastier.' Mario grinned mischievously. 'Wait 'ere, I'll go and git me fishin' tackle an' me gun I suppose, case them fish don' bite.'

'Don' 'e let Ma see 'e.'

'Don't worry Son, I'll just say us is goin' to the village shop.' Mario brow creased. 'On second thoughts us ain't 'lowed in there, is us?'

Marco anticipating yet another outburst, stood watching and waiting for Mario to re-emerge from the wagon. Mario reappeared unruffled. 'Dinna 'ave to say anthin', he told him on his approach, 'er wun 'round, 'er must 'ave gone out.'

Mario freed of his encumbrances, tapped his clay pipe on the bark of a tree, and put it in his pocket. 'Well son, do 'e want to come?' He cried, 'if so git a move on, the fish are there, fer the takin'.' Picking up his tackle and shouldering his shot gun, he crunched towards the stream, Marco and the dog on his heels.

'By the way,' Mario said, as they stepped into a cool leafy woodland interior 'this time, us 'ad best keep to the woods, not go through the village, else us might bump into that 'orrible woman. Wot's 'er name?'

Charlie says, 'er names Mildred Marsh. 'er don' like gypsies, I dunno why.'

'Wot a name,' scoffed Mario, 'and wot a woman!'

∽✏∾

CHAPTER 11

M a!' 'Ma!' A voice broke the silence.
'Whatever's the time?' Harry switched on the bedside light, his eyes blinked with the glow.
Iris yawned and rubbed her eyes. 'It sounds like Charlie, I'd better go and see what's wrong.'

'What now, at this unearthly hour?' Harry glanced at the bedroom clock. 'I've work in the morning.'

'Yes now,' Iris replied dogmatically. 'It's not like him, something's wrong.' She slipped on her woollen dressing gown and mules then made for the door. Downstairs the clock struck three. She padded across the landing. From outside Charlie's bedroom door on seeing a chink of light, she paused. 'Charlie, are you awake?' She called in a subdued voice. 'It's Ma.' With no response, she opened the door a crack and peeped in.

In the glow of the bedside light, Charlie could be seen sitting up in bed. His face ashen, he clutched the sheet, and stared into space.

'Whatever's wrong?' Iris asked.

At the sound of her voice, he turned and looked at her. 'Nothin', he replied woodenly. 'Can I 'ave a drink of water?'

'Charlie, you can tell me, I'm your mother.' Alarm bells ringing, she sat down on the edge of the bed. 'What's troubling you? A trouble shared is a trouble halved.'

''e'll think I'm bein' silly.'

'I won't, you'll see.' Iris searched his face for clues. 'Just try me.' Charlie's tremulous voice frightened her. Puzzled she asked, 'What are you afraid of?'

'One minite, 'e wos dead an' 'orrible jest as us saw 'im, then 'e wos alive.'

'Charlie you're not making sense. It sounds like you've had a nightmare.' Iris placed a comforting hand on his shoulder. 'I'm not surprised under the circumstances. I'll get you a nice milky drink, that should help you to get back to sleep.' She lifted her hand from his shoulder, and stood up. 'Poor Oscar, your Dad and I were upset too. He was such a lovely dog. But now he's out of his misery. Time will heal.'

Quite out of character a concerned Charlie, pulled at her sleeve. 'But Ma! You don' understand, t'wasn't Oscar, 'e's dead, but an alive dog. 'e wos grey and long legged.'

Iris smiled. 'It's just a nightmare.' She ruffled his hair. 'You're tired, you're getting all mixed up. Once you've had your milk, try and get some sleep. Things will look better in the morning.'

Charlie mustered up a smile. 'Can I 'ave me drink, now.'

'Right, I'll get it for you,' said Iris, happier to see him in a calmer state of mind. 'Then settle down, your Dad and I have a busy day ahead of us tomorrow.'

'What's the matter?' asked Harry on her return.

'Nothing really,' said Iris, 'Charlie's so impressionable and the way he found Oscar's body was just too much for him, I really don't know who he turns after. On hindsight we shouldn't have had that burial service.'

'You suggested it.' Harry reached out to switch out the light. 'Who's worrying now?'

Wide awake Iris stared into the darkness. 'But Harry, we couldn't have left Oscar alone in those grounds, he deserved a decent send off, even though he's just a dog.'

To this there was no reply, just a gentle snore.

Even with Ma's advice and a hot drink, deep in thought, Charlie couldn't sleep. Bleary eyed the next morning, he watched Iris load the washing machine.

'Snap out of it Charlie.' Iris straightened her back, wiped her hands on her wrap-over. 'Find something to do, there's plenty, I should know.'

'I'll take a walk.' Charlie didn't want to exasperate her.

'Good idea.' Iris set the timer and the machine in motion. 'Perhaps the fresh air will do you good.'

Outside, Charlie sat swinging his legs on the stone wall by the garden gate. He glanced up and down the road. It was quiet.

Across the road, a man queued at the bus stop, behind him two women with shopping baskets gossiped. In the distance, a girl he knew vaguely, walked her dog. He racked his brain. What was her name?

Adjacent, the church clock picked up a momentum, whirred and struck the hour, it's sonorous sounds broke the silence. Charlie glanced at his watch, to his dismay finding it was only nine o'clock. He hadn't really wanted to go for a walk; he just said he would to keep the peace.

Not a soul to be seen, Charlie was bored. Gerry Pearce had the newspaper round, or thought he had, but not now with the closure of the village store. And what happened to Marco? Some friend, he'd turned out to be, making off into the night. Everything had come to an abrupt halt. A grimy village shop front. No house to house inquiries. Now no-one even seemed interested in the gypsies. It was almost as if they had never existed. Had that horrible Mildred Marsh vanished off the face of the earth? Strangely enough, at that moment, he heard the sound of a vehicle. Was it the bus at last? The man at the bus stop looked hopeful. A taxi suddenly materialised, travelling at speed. As it passed by he managed to catch a glimpse of it's passenger. The face at the window was that of Mildred Marsh. Had she spotted him? Where was she going in such a hurry?

Charlie closed his eyes, in an attempt to block out a mental image of the expression on her face, one he choose not to remember. On opening them again, he was to find he was not alone. Above him perched on a branch was a magpie. Head on one side, it eyed him curiously, before taking to the air with a whirr of wings. He watched it in graceful flight, until coming to rest on the church roof.

Having lost interest, he jumped down from the wall, with no idea of where he was going or what he was going to do.

⚭

CHAPTER 12

Mildred Marsh awoke to a dawn chorus. She was trembling, but at first didn't know why. She eased herself from her bed. Drew back the curtains and peeped out the window. Everything was normal; birds twittered in the hedgerows, a cat was prowling. Then the horrors of her nightmare, took shape.

There they were in the courtroom, symbols of normality, in stark contrast to the nightmare, fragments of which in the cold light of day she still recalled such as the scornful expression on the gypsy's face, when she'd encountered him in the church porch. Even with the passage of time, the thought of his dark eyes still mesmerised her. Now a judge, that same gypsy wore a powdered wig. The jury, all gypsies, their dark eyes mocked, they chanted discordantly, 'Sentence first … trial afterwards.' Standing in the dock, she'd searched for words. Dumbfounded and faint, she'd reached out for a support, but found none. She screamed as suddenly falling deep down into a dark abyss, at the bottom of which the bloodied Colonel had lain.

For a while Mildred lay on her back on the old iron bedstead, staring up at the low whitewashed ceiling where a spider was in the process of spinning a web. In the little box room under the eaves she had always felt safe. Her sanctuary, in times of trouble, a place she had shared with her sister as a child, with so many memories. An image of her sister's face as she remembered it, brought an inward glow: reverting to type, Mildred there and then hatched a plan of action.

A moment or two later outside in the taxi she snapped open her handbag, rifled in her purse for loose change, adjusted her hat, and settled down in the back seat. Condensation obscured the side window. With a gloved hand, she wiped the glass and peered out.

Not many villagers were up and about, thank goodness, to witness her hurried departure, but Charlie Blackmore sitting on the stone wall outside his cottage. What was he doing up so early? She wondered. Up to no good, I'll be bound. At the bus stop, a man with a worried expression on his face, paced impatiently up and down, two women with shopping baskets gossiped.

Mildred hadn't seen her sister, Maud, for years and didn't know what to expect. Still under the circumstances, with the robbery at the Gables still on everyone's lips, she had little alternative, for she knew of no other place to go, and it was necessary to keep a low profile.

On her arrival at the railway station, Mildred took a seat in the waiting room. With her few possessions by her side, she idly listened to what she considered the moronic exchanges between early morning stragglers. Apprehensive about the outcome of her proposed visit and bored with their incessant chatter, she picked up her suitcase and made her way to the edge of the platform. There she glanced down the railway line listening out intently, for any sign or sound of the train. She didn't have to wait long. Soon the familiar chuff, chuff could be heard, as the train emerging from the darkened tunnel with a hiss of brakes, came to rest at the edge of the platform. And with the passengers having alighted, along with the stragglers and latecomers, she boarded the train.

To her relief, for she wished to remain inconspicuous, she found an empty compartment but not for long. The carriage door swung open to reveal that of an elderly cleric. With one foot already on the running board, he asked. 'Do you mind if I share?'

Ruefully, she shook her head. She watched as he bent down to pick up a suitcase. Now where, she wondered, had he sprung from? She hadn't seen him with the others on the platform.

'I was in the next compartment,' he informed her as if reading her mind when settling down in a corner seat. 'It was a bit noisy, I thought you wouldn't mind.'

But I do mind, she thought. After placing her luggage beside his on an overhanging rack, she sat down. She smiled in response, then averted her eyes, simulating an overzealous interest in a magazine. A pretence short lived.

The Cleric coughed. 'Excuse me, my dear, do you live around here? I saw you get in at the Nettlebridge station, so I wondered.'

'I … I,' for a moment, Mildred flustered by such an unexpected intrusion, replied guardedly, 'Yes, why?'

'Well I know the Vicar, a Rev. Ralph …' The Cleric paused. Scratching his head, he frowned. 'O silly me,' he murmured.

'Watson?'

'Yes that's it, Watson.' The Cleric's eyes lit up. 'Now I remember. But I do feel guilty. He's relatively new to the Parish and I like to visit and encourage. I hope he has settled down with his wife and daughter, it was a daughter, wasn't it?' He sighed. 'Whatever it was, now, I just don't have the time.'

Mildred nodded in agreement, then buried her head behind the magazine. For the rest of the journey, to her relief, they travelled in silence.

On her eventual arrival, Mildred reached for her suitcase, and bidding her travelling companion an abrupt goodbye, alighted. Hurrying across the platform, she stopped for a moment and glanced back at the waiting train. Had she caught a glimpse of a shadowy figure watching her from the compartment window. Or was it just a figment of her imagination?

'Pull yourself together, Mildred,' she muttered. True to form, she adjusted her hat and straightened her skirt. She glanced at the station clock, picked up her suitcase and head held high, made her way purposely through the turnstile, where once outside she hailed a taxi.

Her sister's terraced house was just as she remembered it. Climbing up the newly scrubbed steps, Mildred grasped the highly polished chrome knocker, the one that she always remembered seeing her reflection in, and rapped on the mahogany door. A twitch of the creamy lace curtains in the bay window, gave a fleeting impression of a face. The door opened and she found herself face to face with her sister.

'Oh … it's you!' Maud exclaimed, eyeing her up and down. 'You've aged, and wherever did you get that hat?'

Taken aback by her attitude, Mildred at first didn't respond. She knew there had not been much love lost between her and her twin sister, but such coldness and indifference, even she had not envisaged.

'I … I thought, you'd be pleased to see me,' she stammered. 'You look well.'

Maud's tone hardened, bitterly she commented, 'Why should I be pleased, you never cared about Eddie and I. Didn't even write a letter or send a card. He's dead now, bless him.' She wiped away a remorseful tear. 'And you …' She pointed an accusing finger. 'You, didn't even come to the funeral.'

Mildred flinched. 'I … I didn't know,' she uttered tentatively.

'Didn't care, more like. After I wrote to you too.' Maud sniffed. 'Still I've made my own life now, you've got to, you know.'

'I'm sorry.' Mildred didn't know what else to say.

'And so you should be!' Maud's concentration was wavering. Puzzled, she asked, 'Anyway, why are you here?'

This isn't the right time, Mildred thought, but nevertheless asked, 'I was wondering if for a short time I …'

'You can't stay here, if that's what you were going to ask,' cried Maud, her grey eyes, so like Mildred's, flashing defiantly. 'I'm not a Bed & Breakfast Establishment. If that's what you want, there's one just down the road.'

As far as Mildred was concerned, such a remark was uncalled for, so with eyes lowered, she turned on her heel to go.

'Wait!' The sound of Maud's voice was like music to her ears. Had she imagined it, or had her sister's tone changed. She turned, her eyes questioning.

'I shall be going out, but you can come in for a moment for a cup of tea or coffee, if you wish.' Maud managed a smile.

As Maud bustled around in the back kitchen, Mildred sat gingerly on the edge of a leather settee in the little front room. Everything was just as she remembered it, not a thing out of place. She buried her aching feet in the deep-piled Axminster carpet. A victim of arthritis, she would have done anything to take of her shoes.

The room smelling of furniture polish was silent, but for the steady tic of a French Carriage Clock on the marble mantelpiece, beside which stood a silver framed photograph of a young and carefree Eddie. Nearby, propped up on an highly polished bureau by the half opened window, an ornate framed wedding photograph, beside it another of their grandchildren, now grown up. Her sister, so like herself in looks, she had to admit had worn well, despite the ravages of time.

She stood up and casually glanced at her image in a mirror suspended from the chimney breast and despaired. The same couldn't be said for her. Reproachful grey eyes met hers, set back in a thinner face, pallid and wrinkled, with a mouth in a firm line. She was now beginning to look what she had become a blackmailer, a robber and a potential killer. But was the Colonel dead, had she really killed him? What would she do if she had, where would she go? For her there would be no hiding place.

Eddie unlike Maud, had always been good natured and would never have turned her away, whatever she had done. A sense of sadness enveloped her when she thought of her own loveless and childless marriage. 'Why ... why,' she questioned, 'Had the fates been so unkind?'

'You can come and visit me again, if you want to, but please let me know.' Maud laid a sympathetic hand on her shoulder. As their eyes met, had there been Mildred wondered, the suggestion of a tear in her sister's eyes?

With a mixture of emotions, Mildred mustered up a smile, barely aware of Maud's presence on the steps, she waved goodbye. Head bent, with a heavy heart she set off for the station.

'Roses, Carnations, any flower your heart desires.' A fresh-faced woman at the station turnstile selling flowers greeted her with a ready smile. 'Three pence for a bunch of violets.'

Mildred paused, picking up a bunch, she held it against her cheek. Homeward bound, in an empty compartment, she glanced at the violets lying in her lap. She had been well aware, as she waved goodbye, that she would never see her twin sister again. But those last few minutes on the steps, like the posy she had bought so impulsively, as far as she was concerned, had reinforced the bond they had always had between them, one that never could be broken, no matter what happened.

Even so, for her now a bleak prospect lay ahead. A lonely existence, with the finger of suspicion for ever pointing in her direction. In a melancholy mood, she gazed out at the rolling countryside, basking in the late morning sun. The rhythm of the train spurred her on, she searched her mind for an answer to her dilemma, finding none, she prayed fate would take a hand.

∝∞∝

CHAPTER 13

Barefoot, Marco followed his father into the wood, the mottled grey dog running on ahead. In its dim interior, they picked their way along a network of narrow paths, now partially obscured by a riotous tangle of brambles, stinging nettles, long grasses and wild flowers, over a carpet of dead leaves, soft mosses, wet and velvety to the feet, in an atmosphere in which bees hummed and birds chirped where a smell not unlike garlic prevailed. Overhead light breezes stirred a green leafy canopy. Branches and leaves shimmered and rustled, in the shadows. Bizarre shapes danced on tree trunks upon which ingrained, the stems of Hedge Bindweed twined its large white trumpet shape flowers. A woodland world, with an indiscernible smell of summer, vibrating with sights and sounds, patches of sunlight, picking out Dog's Mercury, St. Johns Wort, Dog Violets and other wild flowers, around which bees buzzed and flies swarmed.

Running on ahead, the swarthy gypsy boy's dark eyes lit up when hearing a curious rattling sound made by a Great Spotted Woodpecker, drumming vigorously at dead wood. By his side, the dog with the lure of a rabbit, plunged into the tangled undergrowth to sniff at a burrow, but the rabbits were snug below ground. Nearby, a buff-tailed bumblebee having build its nest underground probably in an old burrow made by a mouse or vole, buzzed around the violet blue bell-shaped flowers of a hairy perennial. Fascinated, Marco stopped and watched it. Woodland wonders such as these filled him with awe. On his way up the path, on one side, parting back the leafy foliage, he caught a glimpse of biscuit-coloured pastureland drenched in sunshine. On a tree lined bank a handful of cows swished their tails, as they drank from a stream, that gurgled and glistened in the sun, some lying in the shade.

Now, a little way ahead, Mario tired and hungry paused and laid down his fishing tackle. His stomach rumbled. The dog tired of foraging was hungry too; soft brown eyes searched the gypsy's face.

'I 'aven't got anythin', Ole Boy.' Mario's grimy, calloused hand ruffled the dog's silky ears, 'e'll 'ave to wait.' The dog once more raced ahead, picking up a scent.

'Ah, there 'e is,' Mario muttered, as Marco caught him up. 'Where 'ave 'e bin?' He picked up his fishing tackle. 'I wos 'bout to go on without 'e.'

'I'm 'ungry, did 'e bring anythin' to eat?'

'Not a bite, Son, I forgot.' Mario took off his tattered old cap, and scratched his head. 'T'was your Ma. 'er puts me off, goin' on like 'er does 'bout little Juanita. Us'll 'ave to bag a pheasie or a fish, light a fire an' …'

Marco's spirits soared.

For a while the Romanies cleared the way ahead in silence. Stinging nettles, brambles, and dank grasses vied for survival. The path wound deeper into the wood. Mario paused when hearing the long descending song of a wood warbler. It was a good omen.

He straightened his aching back. He wiped the perspiration of his face with the back of his hand.

'Feelin' tired?'

Mario didn't reply. He looked around. 'Where's the dog?'

The dog lagging behind, whined.

Marco's mind switched back to his first encounter with Charlie, his friend from the village. Charlie's look of despair as he'd knelt over the injured dog wondering what to do. Marco had always thought of the dog as Charlie's, even though he had named him 'Rover' still Charlie could change the name. Where was Charlie now? He wondered, and what was he doing, should he have left him? As usual he felt a sense of guilt and despondency.

'That Mildred woman, wud 'e say 'er's mad, Marco?' Mario's gruff voice to his relief, interrupted these thoughts.

''er names Mildred Marsh.' Marco was not surprised to hear Mario once again refer to 'that Mildred woman.' But hoped his Dad wouldn't spend the next hour or two with endless recriminations, for Mario had never got over his confrontation with Mildred in the church porch and nearly always raised the subject. As far as he was concerned he'd lost face, quite unforgivable for a gypsy, especially in front of a woman. It had become an obsession. Many a time, he had gone over what he should have said and how at the time.

'I ain'seen 'er close up, but 'er's got a 'orrible temper, so Charlie says.'

'Charlie, yer mate?'

Relieved, Marco seized the change of topic. 'I miss 'im.' He looked down despondently at the tangled mass of greenery they'd just cleared. 'I shouldn't 'ave left 'im, but Ma …'

'Yer Ma's bossy when 'er's on 'er 'igh 'orse.' Mario smiled sympathetically, and patted Marco on the shoulder. Although not so robust as Marco, Mario too had quite taken to the fair haired, pale faced village boy. As always, he felt a warm glow when he compared Charlie with his son. Marco filled him with pride with his unruly mop of black hair and winning ways, but there was no reasoning with Eliza, she was so stubborn. Mario mused, a sudden thought prompting him to ask. 'By the way, that night at the big 'ouse did 'e 'ear a woman screamin'?'

'Yes,' replied Marco puzzled by the query, especially as such a time had elapsed. 'Why?'

'Nothin', did 'e see anythin' else?'

'No I told 'e jest a green van in a 'urry, ain't us goin' fishin'? Marco tired and hungry wished to change the subject.

'Yes son, wot's that?' Mario paused, he listened intently as from the depths of the wood, came the unmistakable cry of a pheasant. 'Us'll be eatin' soon.' He winked.

Marco grinned in response, he licked his lips.

Rover was his old self again. He picked up a scent, wagged his tail, his long hairy body quivered. Without warning he plunged into the tangled undergrowth.

'Tis the pheasie!' exclaimed Mario, 'Listen! As unseen from a distance, a frantic barking rose to a crescendo, followed by a startled cry.

'I wonder,' said Mario, wiping his brow.

'Wot?' Not Mildred Marsh again, Marco thought.

'Will us 'ave pheasie or fish?'

After a while the path widened, they came upon a clearing where Rover had found a temporary resting place, beside a fallen tree trunk. Beside him on the grass lay an assortment of feathers, the victims remains, the only sign left of its battle for survival. The dog unperturbed by Mario's cool indifference, got up and wagged his tail vigorously.

'Since the dogs 'as 'ad e's fill, and left us not even a morsel,' Mario commented. 'Fishin' it 'tis.' He eyed Rover contemptuously. 'But I think I'll take a leaf out of 'es book an' rest a while.'

Mario lay down his fishing tackle, squat down with his back against the grainy tree trunk and with a sigh of contentment, closed his eyes. Tentatively, a contrite Rover edged slowly towards him and poked a wet muzzle in his face.

'Wot the … git off! Mario's raised voice sent Rover romping to the other side of the copse, where Marco had just spotted a stagnant pool infested with myriad flies and insects.

'The pool pongs.' Marco said, looking down at a still slimy green surface pitted with dead insects. He screwed up his face in disgust. 'It's mucky, an' full of 'orrible things, us best move on.'

'Wot now?' Reluctant to get up, Mario's eyes widened.

'Us 'ave only just got 'ere. Can't a man 'ave a bit of peace? I wos thinkin' of havin' a nap.'

'No not 'ere. Wot would Ma say.'

''er's always sayin' somethin' Mario snorted. 'But 'er won't know will 'er? Still 'tis best us moves on, since 'e says the pools mucky.'

Further on, stepping out from the leafy shelter of the wood, Mario laid down his fishing tackle and lit up his old clay pipe, for a while momentarily mesmerized, by it's effect. Marco standing by his side, surveyed the outlying area, contented, Rover stretched then sprawled in the long grasses. Before them lay a vast panorama of fields dotted with cattle, sheep and farmland. A vista through which a stream meandered sparkling in the sunshine, the distant sound of a tractor could be heard, and where up, up in a cloudless sky, a kestrel, poised hovering, it's sharp eyes monitoring the precise place where it would swoop upon a un-suspecting field mouse.

Taken by surprise, Rover let out a stifled bark, when close at hand a raucous caw revealed the presence of a rook perched on the branches of a sycamore tree. With a sudden whirr of wings, a juicy worm dangling from it's beak, it took to the air, soon no more than a speck in the sky.

Drawn to the loud 'strich-stritch call of swifts high overhead, and the 'vitt vitt' or dsched-dsched of numerous swallows attract-ed by flies swarming around grazing sheep, Mario commented as much to himself as to Marco, 'One swallow don' make a sum-mer … so 've' 'eard.'

'Wot Mario? Wot be goin' on 'bout?'

'Folks say, one swallow don' make a summer … A Bohemi-an one? But there ain't any fear of that.'

Disturbed by the activity, a white admiral, feeding on the nectar from a bramble blossom, fluttered butterfly wings of vi-brant black and white, and took to the air.

'Bohemian?' Marco queried, glancing again at the swallows and swifts.

'Free, son, free. I read it in a book. A free life, free to roam.' Mario's eyes took on a faraway look. 'One that your Ma, Grand-ma and our Ancestors 'ad, a life comin' to an end.' Overcome with emotion, he brushed away a tear.

Marco averted his eyes. He had never known his Dad to show weakness.

'If it 'appens will us be put in jail?' Marco visualised a con-crete cell with bars on the window. A frugal life with only bread and water.

'Not if I can 'elp it son,' Mario sniffed, giving himself a men-tal shake, his voice hardened. 'But that's 'nough of that, us were supposed to be goin' fishin.'

Compared to the shady woodland they had left behind, the open countryside that lay before them, exposed to the fierce rays of the sun, soon became blanketed in a heat haze.

'I saw somethin'. Marco pointed to a spot in the wide expanse of meadowland.

'Wot?' Mario screwed up his eyes, with his hand shielding them from the brightness.

'No, 'e be lookin' in the wrong direction ... there.'

Mario focused his eyes, this time looking in the direction to which Marco pointed, through the heat haze seeing a figure emerge, that of a young boy.

'It's Charlie!' Marco couldn't believe it, he was ecstatic.

Like a shot from a gun, the dog, his senses aroused, left their side and romped across the field, an uncanny instinct leading him straight to the lone figure. Witnessing what they thought a joyful reunion between boy and dog, Mario turning to Marco commented, 'That's 'ow 'e met, 'an that's 'ow 'e'll meet again.'

◦◈◦

'Ouch.' Another bramble hidden in the long grasses impeded Charlie's progress, tentatively, he separated it's tenacious grasp from his well-worn denims, in so doing, it had sprung back and brushed against his arm. But this was the least of his concerns, a momentary annoyance, which only added to the many stings and scratches he had acquired in a relatively short space of time. Now not an attractive image, with his dismal expression, a grubby knotted handkerchief covering his head, a muddied t-shirt and denims, clinging to his sweaty torso, he stopped and wiped beads of perspiration off his forehead with the back of his hand, before glancing up at a blazing sun.

Charlie was fascinated by the heat haze, for he couldn't remember ever having seen anything like it. All around him it lay like a mantel of snow. It enveloped the field and the distant countryside, as far as the eye could see, creating a world of mist with ghostlike images. Through this soporific atmosphere alone, unnoticed, as he thought, he passed, finding it a tranquil place where lulled, birds and creatures were asleep or subdued, an equilibrium soon to be broken by the sound of a distant tractor.

Feeling hungry and lethargic, his thoughts turned to home and one of Ma's pies. He conjured up a picture of one, straight from the oven, the pastry brown and crisp, filled with succulent meat, smothered in gravy. He could almost smell the aroma, savour the taste, his tummy rumbling as if in agreement. In the larder, there had been plenty of food and a pie, but not sure of his intentions, he hadn't taken any. Now with hindsight he realised his mistake. If he had only brought a bottle of pop or an apple.

He was beginning to realise the school holidays were not all they were cracked up to be. For now alone and without Marco, he felt despondent and aimless and in such abominable heat, so tired.

When pondering as he frequently did about the robbery at the Gables, and Marco's sudden disappearance, he'd mutter to an unseen audience, 'Wot did I do wrong, nothin'.' What if his gypsy friend had panicked, in the heat of the moment lost his nerve, left him to face the music? Why should he be the one, made to feel like a criminal?

Charlie paused for breath, rummaging in his pockets, he had hoped to find a leftover sweet or chew but to his chagrin, found only a length of string, and a forgotten pea shooter. Momentarily, he toyed with the latter, then disappointed pocketed it with his fruitless haul. His feet sore with blisters, raw with rubbing, he took off his new trainers, tied them together and looped them around his neck. He'd had enough, he was going home.

He was making up his mind which way to go back, when aware of a presence, he saw the flicker of a movement, a temporary parting in the long grasses, as nearing something panting. Was it a snake? He asked himself. Couldn't be, snakes didn't pant. A sheep or a cow? In the mist and long grasses who could tell, although a cow was large enough, surely. Rooted to the spot he held his breath, wondering what to expect but not for long.

The mottled grey wolfhound, his pink tongue lolling from side to side, breathless from his previous exertions, padded down the overgrown footpath towards Charlie. It was the same dog that he had rescued. The one that along with Marco and Mario,

Marco's Dad, he'd taken to the gypsy encampment. 'Marco's Ma sed,'e'd be as right as rain, 'an 'e is.' Charlie cried, delighted to see him again.

The bedraggled creature didn't seem to recognise him nor share his enthusiasm. Neither did he jump up, but seemed surprised as Charlie with the unexpected encounter.

'Suppose, like Marco 'e's made off?' As if in response the dog thumped his tail. 'You come 'ome with me, I'll 'ide 'e in the shed.'

The dog barked, with a submissive look, sinking down on all fours.

''e don' fancy that.' Charlie started to walk away.

For a while the dog watched him, then rising on his haunches, started to pad purposely off up the path in the direction of the woods.

Although still hungry, Charlie overcome with curiosity, bare-footed, followed him, all thoughts of Ma's pie forgotten.

With Charlie straggling behind, they hadn't gone far when the dog bounding ahead, stopped abruptly. Raising his head, sniffing the air, he pricked up his ears, the very next moment as if on cue, vanishing from sight amongst the long grasses. Charlie on reaching the spot where he had disappeared, stood there and whistled in vain. The dog had been distracted. But, by what? Perhaps, nose down, by now he had picked up a scent, the track of a rabbit, hare or mouse, bird scent from a partridge.

In a humid atmosphere, the field baked. Tired and by now very hungry, Charlie stumbled on towards the woods where having reached it's leafy interior, he succumbed to an all embracing coolness. His eyes having adjusted to the dim interior, he glanced around. There were many paths, dividing, subdividing and merging in it's depths, some apparently leading nowhere. Most of these, partially hidden in a tangle of brambles and stinging nettles, with a drone or buzz of myriad insects from within. He made his way over a woodland floor carpeted with ferns, mosses, and wood anemones, in an atmosphere heavy with a pungent smell akin to garlic, where as in the field, the birds and creatures were in repose but in a tranquil shadowy haven.

It was then he saw a creature. The stoat coming face to face, hissed, then just as it had suddenly appeared, swiftly vanished. Already on edge, Charlie jumped when taken unawares by a sudden movement seemingly in a clump of bracken. Was it the wolfhound? He hoped so. It was a pity the dog had run away. But it wasn't, it was a squirrel. Wide-eyed, it emerged and scampered across the path just in front of him, scaling the nearest tree. A surprise phenomenon, prompting him to stand by the trunk to look up into the leafy canopy. The next moment, an acorn whizzed through the air. He heard a chuckle, at first seeing no-one then partially camouflaged a figure. Perched on one of the highest branches of the old oak tree, a familiar sight with a mop of black hair and an impish grin.

'It can't be, it is!' he gasped. 'Marco, wot yer doin' up there?'

'Nothin', jest watchin' 'e tryin' to bag a squirrel fer yer supper'.

'Ugh, I couldn't eat a squirrel, if I wos starvin'. But ...' Anxious blue eyes met a pair of mischievous dark ones. 'Marco where 'ave ...'

'Bin 'ere and there,' the gypsy boy remarked carelessly. He swung his legs, with the motion, the branch rocking precariously. His sunburnt face creased with laughter when seeing Charlie's horrified expression. Almost losing his balance, he exclaimed, 'Bet 'e thought t'wos the squirrel!' His eyes glowed. 'My yer face, 'e looked so...' Again he laughed, this time holding his sides. The branch shook.

Charlie watching with a mixture of horror, mingled with a sense of relief, at seeing his pal again, cried. 'Marco, min' 'e don' fall.'

'Fall, wot me? Marco taking a deep breath, puffed out his chest. 'e must be jokin' or forgotten to whom you'm talkin' to. It's Marco, I'm back!' Then with a touch of humility, 'That's if yer wants me.'

Charlie's broad smile spoke volumes. 'Of course I want you. But I'm so 'ungry. I wos thinkin' of goin' 'ome, that is 'til I saw the dog.'

'Don' 'e worry 'bout 'im. 'e'll find e's way back. There's no need to go 'ome, Da's fishin' downstream.' Sliding down the knotted trunk, Marco landed at his feet. 'Comin'?'

'Wot 'bout the dog?' Charlie pulled a face.

Marco shrugged his shoulders. 'Like I said, 'e'll find 'es way. 'e'll probably turn up covered in muck, like 'e usually does when 'e's 'ungry.'

Unconvinced, Charlie remarked, 'But wot if 'e gits lost.'

''Tis no loss.' Marco commented drily. 'There's plenty where 'e comes from.'

Reluctantly Charlie followed Marco down the path. He wasn't so sure.

⊷⊷

Mario cushioned on a grassy knoll by the stream, drew contentedly on his old clay pipe. In finding the shady copse, he had found a temporary sanctuary from the fierce rays of the sun, a place where he could sit in solitude and dream with his makeshift rod and line.

Soothed by the gentle lapping of the water, whipped up by a breeze downstream, Mario sat there at first thinking of nothing in particular. Beside him the wolfhound yawned and stretched. Enjoying such peaceful surroundings, he ruffled the animal's ears, the dog closed his eyes in ecstasy.

Mario puffed away, idly observing spirals of hazy blue smoke rising and dispersing, momentarily at peace with the world, until he chanced to think of Mildred what's her name? Marco had told him the woman's name, but he had blanked it out.

In the distance, the muted clickety-clack of a train, stirred his imagination, conjuring up a mental picture of the passengers, people always on the move. His mind switched back to the conversation he had had with his son in the quiet shady woods. At that time, baring his soul, he had strengthened his resolve, for weren't places such as this, in which he now found himself, where animals and humans could live as nature intended, indeed special … a what was it? 'Oh yes,' he voiced aloud. 'A Bohemian Way of Life.' The dog lying at his feet, as if in agreement, whimpered.

Even so, Mildred what's her name, still intruded on his thoughts, in this peaceful place. A gypsy from a long lineage, Mario although somewhat naïve, was proud of his way of life and unable to grasp anyone's aversion to it.

The drone of a light aircraft dispelling these flights of fancy, prompted Mario to shade his eyes and look up. From the direction of the woods, like a silver bird glistening in the sun's rays, the plane appeared over the treetops. Up in the clear blue sky, it dipped it's wings, banked then flew low over fields barely visible in the heat haze. Mario stood up and watched it climb, distant itself, become just a speck then no more.

The dog poised on the edge of the bank, caught sight of a movement in the sunlit waters of the stream, barking, he wagged his tail, as with a sudden disturbance, the fishing line curved under a strain. Beside him, Mario speedily reeled in the catch. A trout splashing and thrashing around on the grass, at last conceded defeat. The gypsy's spirits lifted. Pleased with his prize, he searched the coppice, for kindling.

With a gas lighter, Mario ignited a nest of dried wood and grasses. Soon a thin spiral of smoke with the semblance of a flame appeared. This he fanned diligently setting it ablaze. With strong sticks, he fashioned crosses, placing them on either side of the fire, between which he placed a crossbar, from which with a sharp knife having gutted the fish, he suspended on a hook, watched by the dog, his open jaws drooling in anticipation.

On the grassy slope, Mario lay resting on one elbow, watching fingers of flame, lick and dance around the fish, from it a tantalising smell setting off his gastric juices. His hands sticky and messy he wiped them in an old rag, he'd brought for the purpose. He closed his eyes listening to the rustle of the leaves, now and then opening them to keep a watchful eye on the dog, sprawling perilously near to the edge of the fire.

'Ain't that a sight fer sore eyes!' Marco standing close to the fire, prodded the glowing embers with a stick.

On hearing the familiar voice, the gypsy opened his eyes. 'Oh it's you,' he retorted, 'where 'ave 'e bin?'

'Talkin' to Charlie.'

Just behind Marco, lost for words, stood a tentative Charlie, his face expressionless, although lightening up, when catching sight of the dog.

'Come closer, lad I won't bite 'e'. Mario's gruff voice did little to allay Charlie's fears. 'ungry?'

'Yes Sir.'

Marco grinned. 'e's worrid 'bout the dog. I told him there's plenty where 'e's ...'

'Never mind 'bout that.' Mario's stomach rumbled. 'Sit down, let's 'ave some grub.'

'Ain't 'e a good cook,' Marco and Charlie with fingers and thumbs, picked at a portion of fish on makeshift plates fashioned from large leaves with relish.

Scoffing down his in no time, Mario eyeing Charlie, exclaimed. 'Mind the dog, 'e's got 'is eye on yer plate. Wot 'ave 'e bin doin' wi' yerself?' He asked, trying to draw a rather subdued Charlie.

'Nothin' much, Sir' said Charlie. 'Since ...'

'That night, 'e means the one at the big 'ouse,' broke in Marco.

'Let 'im speak for 'imself, 'e's got a tongue, 'asn't 'e?' retorted Mario. 'Well Charlie, anythin' special?'

Searching for something to say, Charlie responded, 'Nothin' 'cept, buryin' Oscar, the Colonel's dog with me Ma and Dad. Us found 'im under an old Oak behin' the big 'ouse.' 'e wos in a terrible state, flies an' all that.' Charlie wiped away a remorseful tear. 'Ma wanted it done proper, it being a Sunday, wi' a cross and some flowers an' all that. Us said prayers over 'im.'

'And that Mildred wot's 'er name? Wot's 'er up to, now?' Mario leant forward, all ears.

'Dunno, I saw 'er in a taxi this mornin.' said Charlie, wiping his sticky hands in Mario's old rag. 'er didn't look 'appy.'

Mario frowned. 'Is 'er ever?'

'No, suppose not.'

Marco was becoming bored, he felt the conversation was leading nowhere, so in an attempt to change it commented. 'T'wasn't 'nuff.' I'm 'ungry and Ma will 'spect a fish supper.'

'spect 'er will. My ain't it hot.' Mario wiped his brow. He sighed. With his gas lighter, he relit his pipe. Puffing away for a few seconds, he remarked as if to himself. 'Fish fer the takin', maybe there is, maybe there ain't.'

With this the conversations tailed off, each one subdued by the sultry atmosphere.

Marco seated in front of the fire, his hands on drawn up knees, stared into the dying embers.

Mario after a while, closed his eyes, his lighted pipe, much to Charlie's consternation, dropping from his grasp. He got up, trying to appear inconspicuous, he snuffed it out, unaware that he was being observed.

'Gie it to me, I'll put it in 'is pocket.' Marco stretched out his hand, took it and saying nothing more, resumed his fireside vigil.

It was so unlike Marco, that Charlie didn't know what to think. Perhaps it was the heat or was he just disappointed with him? Perhaps he had expected some news. Was his friend finding his company boring? He hoped not. Feeling strangely inadequate in their presence, particularly Marco's, he experienced an unexpected emotion, one dispelling all the pleasure, he had once derived, when first encountering Marco. Now and then Charlie glanced at the dog. Content, he lay sprawled in front of the remnants of a dying fire, lost to the world, his ears twitching, that is until the shot rang out.

'Wot the blazes …?' Mario awoke with a start. Adjusting his cap, he sat up and rubbing his eyes, remarked. 'T'was someone takin' a pot shot over there, if I ain't mistaken.' He pointed in the direction of the woods.

'Mario … do 'e think us needs to be worrid?' Asked Marco perplexed. 'Us ain't popular 'round 'ere.'

'Son, 'hose to know.' The gypsy shrugged his shoulders. 'Times are a changin' ain't they? An' wi' that Mildred wots 'er name poisin' folk's minds.' With a defiant look in his dark eyes, he retorted. 'Us Romanies will go our way as us always 'ave, where an' when us wants an' not afore.' He sighed. 'Can't a body be left in peace? … Anyways I ain't goin' to let it worry me.' And with that Mario settling down in his former position, in no time was asleep.

Watching him, Marco's black eyes clouded over and lost their sparkle, for he was convinced of some hidden danger. 'Didn't see a soul, did 'e, Charlie?' he asked tentatively.

'Marco, the dog, 'es made off!' Charlie struggled to find his voice, a voice that seemed strange and far away.

Marco now standing up, his hands in his pockets, scanning the woods, didn't respond at first.

'Did 'e 'ear wot I said?' Charlie persisted, alarmed and surprised at Marco's negative attitude. ''e ran off wi the shot.' Moved by Marco's indifference, he got up and touched him on the shoulder.

'I 'eard,' said Marco, without turning around. 'Let 'im go, 'e'll come back, 'when 'e's of a mind an' 'ungry.'

But Charlie wasn't convinced. 'Suppose … suppose 'e get's shot agin.' he stammered, as he always did under pressure. It didn't bear thinking about.

Marco seeing Charlie's worried expression, although puzzled, felt sorry for him. But merely commented, 'So wot 'es only a dog.'

'No not agin,' murmured Charlie. His mind switched back to the wolfhound lying on the riverbank, his body peppered with shot, oozing with gore.

'It ain't fair, 'e may be dead now, lyin' somewheres.'

'I'll 'elp 'e find 'im.' Marco sighed dispassionately. He caste a sidelong glance at Mario. Eyes tightly shut, mouth wide open, now and then; the traveller emitted a thunderous snore, his body shaking in unison. 'Best leave 'im,' he commented, ''e won't be wake for hours an' 'e only gits 'nnoyed, if 'es woke up… let's make tracks.'

෴

The mist had cleared. Marco wading across the stream, looked back as Charlie clambered down the grassy bank. 'Come on slow-coach …' he hollowed. His voice carrying, a bevy of mallards emerging from some bulrushes, clamoured, flapping their wings. A solitary swan, downstream arched it's neck.

As the afternoon wore on Charlie began to lose heart. To him, since leaving the shelter of the copse, Marco like someone on a mission, seemed blessed with an endless energy, searching every nook and cranny. Always one step ahead, he leapt over dry muddy ditches, climbed overgrown hedges, scoured buttercup fields, stopping now and then to wave him on encouragingly. In one field he encountered a bull, albeit with cows and carried on irrespectively, with a fearful Charlie in tow.

The sun now a golden orb started to slowly sink below the horizon. The two boys, sunburnt and dishevelled, stopped in their tracks on hearing the raucous cries of rooks. Shading their eyes, they stood, and watched the birds wing their way over a countryside basking in a mellow glow, to nests in distant treetops.

'Wot's the time?' Charlie wiping the perspiration from his forehead, with the back of his hand, was beginning to feel hungry again and very thirsty, so much so he scooped up some water from a nearby stream. Ma wouldn't have approved, but at that moment, he didn't care. 'Suppose the water wos contam...' she'd say. What was that word now? A long word, he couldn't remember, it meant dirty. He looked down at his feet, now hardened like Marco's and caked in mud, fingered a tear in his mud stained T-shirt and wondered what she would say. His arms stung as brushing past stinging nettles, an irritation easing with the help of an occasional dock leaf. Bitten by insects, itchy and uncomfortable, the prospect of a bath at that moment, would have been welcomed and not taken begrudgingly, for whenever sitting on his haunches as now, even the occasional scratch with a grubby hand brought no solace.

The robust Marco was not amused. 'Come on, wot do 'e thinks 'es doin,' he cried, his dark eyes scanning a distant pastureland with a backdrop of leafy woodland. 'I dunno' the time or where us is, must 'ave left me timer in the wagon.' The next moment, already under way, he turned and yelled. 'Come on, Charlie!'

Reluctantly, Charlie scrambled to his feet, but soon lagged behind Marco's ever diminishing figure. Disillusioned and hungry, fond though he was of the dog, he regretted having suggested such a fruitless venture. With his head bent against a prevailing wind, he mused. Why was the dog so important? Was it because it was through the mottled grey wolfhound, that he had first met Marco? His mind winged back to that of a boy partially concealed in the overhanging branches of a sycamore tree beside a sunlit stream. Of a boy with the darkest eyes almost as black as his unruly mop of raven black hair, of a boy with a teasing look in his eyes, who exclaimed. 'Wot … ain't 'e seen a gypsy afore!'

Or was it because he missed Oscar, the Colonel's dog? The faithful golden retriever who meant no-one no harm. It wasn't just the shock of finding the old dog in his decomposed state, in the grounds of the Gables, or an ordeal with Ma and Dad's help in burying him, it was something else. The loss of old Oscar had had a profound impact, his very first experience of the death of a loved one.

Shaken from his reverie, by a sudden movement, he turned just in time to see a rabbit shoot across his path. In the split second it looked his way, he glimpsed a be-whiskered face, wide-eyed and panic-stricken. No sooner had it vanished, then to his surprise, in hot pursuit, a familiar shape materialised.

'Charlie, wot's 'e doin' now?' Marco's voice, crystal clear, carried on a rising wind over a wide expanse.

'Marco …' Charlie yelled. 'I can't see 'e.'

'Over 'ere.'

Charlie screwing up his eyes, spotted a far-reaching figure silhouetted against an apricot sky seared with the golden threads of a setting sun. Breathless, he stumbled towards it, eventually coming face to face with a disgruntled Marco.

'The suns dippin', keep movin' or us'll git lost,' the gypsy retorted.

'But Marco.' Charlie gasped

'Wot?' Marco's moody eyes, scrutinized him.

'T'was the dog, I saw 'im. I wasn't dreamin' 'onest.'

'Where?' Marco gave a sceptical look.

'Over there, chasin' a rabbit.' Charlie's eyes indicated a tangled area of scrubland.

'Where's 'e now?'

'Dunno.'

'That ain't any good, come on else I'll 'ave to find 'im on me own.'

The gypsy boy frustrated by Charlie's lack of co-operation soon disappeared over a hillock.

Charlie cupped his hands to his mouth and shouted yet again. 'Marco, ain't 'e waitin' for me … where's 'e gone to?' There was no reply, just the sound of the wind blowing through the long grasses and the distant lowing of cattle. He stood there for a while wondering what to do. The sun had by now disappeared below the horizon. He shivered, his arms with goose pimples, blue with the cold. Under darkening skies, hungry and apprehensive, Charlie had no alternative but to plod on.

In the encroaching darkness, he had just given up all hope, when he spotted the outline of a farm gate. On the other side, the headlights of a vehicle shedding light through its struts, sped past. He felt a sense of relief, quickly dispelled when finding himself in an unknown narrow country lane. He looked this way and that. Go in the same direction of the vehicle, he thought. As he found his way, between gloomy hedgerows, he passed other farm gates, over which an inky starlit void met his eyes.

Sometime later, on rounding a bend, he came across a parked van. Perhaps there would be someone in it. It was too dark to make out it's colour, but he could have sworn it was green. There was something familiar about it. It triggered off a memory, one of a moonlit lane down which he'd seen one disappear. He was tired and afraid. Could he be over reacting? He crept closer and touched the bodywork. On closer examination, gasped. It couldn't be, it was! The metallic green paint with the gold leaf lettering, 'The Nettlebridge Stores, Proprietor, George McDonald was cold to the touch.

The lane quiet, he peered inside. There was a body slumped over the steering wheel. His heart raced. He could hardly breath. Surely not Mr McDonald. He couldn't believe what he was seeing. He rapped on the driver's window. As if in response, the man inside stirred and opened his eyes, glancing in Charlie's direction, he smiled. Charlie gasped. It was Mr. McDonald! He didn't look at all well. Charlie glanced up and down the stony lane. What was he going to do? Stay where he was? Flag down a car? Carry on walking and get help? He didn't know where he was. There wasn't even a signpost. Where was Marco? He could have done with his help, Marco would have known what to do.

Trying to make up his mind, he became aware of a presence. Not knowing what to expect Charlie turned around slowly to be met with a pair of placid brown eyes. It was the wolfhound. Unnoticed, it had been standing in the lane, quietly observing him. As he'd expected, it didn't run away as he slowly moved towards it with an outstretched hand, but wagged his long tail, at the sound of his voice. Charlie was pleased; his pleasure short lived, for now he must find help for the shadowy occupant in the van. Hopefully this time, the dog would choose to stay by his side.

CHAPTER 14

Well Constable, have you found it yet?'

Constable Edward Blackley sensing that the Inspector was in no mood to be trifled with dithered, averting his eyes.

'Well Blackley … have you?' A pragmatist, Inspector Charles Routley, nicknamed 'Charlie' behind his back and sometimes 'a right Charlie', turned and looked at the constable enquiringly.

There followed an uneasy silence, broken, when the constable flustered, his face colouring, murmured, 'I looked through all the files.'

'Speak up man!' The Inspector's eye twitched, a sure sign that he was getting hot under the collar. 'I can hardly hear you.'

Blackley nervously clearing his throat, looked up reluctantly, into the Inspector's steely grey eyes. 'but I …'

'But what?'

Blackley seeing a glint in his eyes, steeled himself, preparing for the accustomed outburst. He clenched his hands.

'Oh I see, it's just what I would expect, you found nothing.' The Inspector shrugging his shoulders, muttered 'Why do I bother?' His patience, that which he possessed, was wearing thin. 'For goodness sake Blackley, stop fidgeting and don't slouch when I'm talking to you.'

'Yes … yes Sir.' The constable wished the floor would swallow him up.

With a cursory look in Blackley's direction, the Inspector frowning, crossed over to the window, and peered out. Outside a bleak prospect met his gaze, a dreary one, with grey skies, misty rain dampening the shrubberies and muddying the footpaths. Here and there in the distance, the proverbial raised umbrella. A swollen river in spate, due to a recent thunderous downpour, raging downstream, under the hump back bridge. The weathers on the change, the Inspector thought, after such a hot spell. Distracted by a discreet cough, he turned to see the constable, standing by his desk. Motivated verbally, he sprung into action. 'Oh it's you Blackley, I quite forgot about you. … Well lad, pull your finger out, and find it now!'

'Yes Sir.' Blackley scurrying off, slammed the door behind him.

The Inspector winced. Moving away from the window sill, he pondered. This particular case seemed to be dragging on and he hated untidy endings, if any at all. The house to house enquiries in Nettlebridge, irksome when shedding no light at the end of a long drawn-out tunnel.

On hearing the screech of brakes, he looked out just in time to see a patrol car pull into the damp forecourt, blue lights flashing. That would be Perkins and Harrison back from traffic control. They had left the lights on yet again, the sight irked him. He would have a word. A thought, short-lived for the Inspector had other matters on his mind, that of an ongoing investigation.

What had really happened at the Gables? Inspector Routley hated mysteries and this current one needled him. Who had robbed and attacked the Colonel, leaving him lying bloodied and near to death on the kitchen's flagstone floor? There might easily have been a breakthrough, that time at the cottage in Nettlebridge. Given time, he might have gleaned some useful information from Charlie Blackmore, the village boy, who lived there, but for the intrusive telephone call from the laboratory, alluding to fingerprints and blood types.

The village constable's account of a loud hammering on the Police House door at 23.00 hours on the night of the robbery, too preyed on his mind. Locked in his brain, the words 'To tell you Mister … a murder at the 'Gables' … Me and Charlie, 'eard it,' uttered by a panic stricken gypsy boy, who fled into the night.

During the course of his investigations, he had concluded that there was no love lost between the villagers and gypsies in a summer encampment on the outskirts. Some said that the finger of suspicion should be pointed in the traveller's direction. Others were concerned with the disappearance of George McDonald, the proprietor of the Nettlebridge General Stores, who apparently had vanished without trace. A bachelor in his mid-forties, once the life and soul of the community, it had been suggested that maybe a woman was involved. That he had to agree would have been a strong motivation. And maybe a sign in the shop front window written in large black capitals, NO GYPSIES SERVED HERE may have contributed to Mr. McDonald's downfall. The sign, in the Inspector's view, an unnecessary provocation, had since been removed. But by whom, when and why? With the shop empty, and rumours rife, the Inspector felt at a loss.

Then there was Mrs Symons, the Colonel's elderly house-keeper. On the surface, she appeared to be a perfectly respecta-ble woman, although when questioned had become agitated. She had implied that the Colonel had kept himself to himself and had hardly said a word to anyone in the village, but for the odd de-rogatory remark in passing about the gypsies. That he had be-come a recluse since the death of his wife in a car accident, cut-ting himself off from village life.

A sitting duck, the Inspector had thought for a random rob-bery from outside the village, living all alone in that big house, but for his dog and the housekeeper, who judging by her atti-tude, may have something to hide.

But now with the re-opening of the case, it was his impera-tive to maintain access to any information; however insignificant.

Mrs Symons had known the owner of the green van. It be-longed to George McDonald, the proprietor of the Nettlebridge General Stores, whose whereabouts was currently unknown. In the past, he had been seen delivering provisions to the 'Gables, on a regular basis. Questioned, the housekeeper's eyes had wid-ened, she'd gasped. 'You don't think he's got anything to do with the robbery, do you?'

Frozen to the spot she'd awaited his reply. A reply that wasn't forthcoming. Something in her manner had triggered off a neg-ative response. Why? Was there a connection between her and the missing storekeeper?

Glancing up at the office clock, the Inspector saw that it was ten o'clock, time for a tea break. But where was Blackley, and whatever was he doing? Enough was enough, he thought, as crossing to his desk. He was just about to lift the telephone receiver, when it shrilled in it's cradle. Now what?

'An outside call from Nettlebridge, I have a Constable Phillips on the line for you Sir,' said the Operator, 'Will you take it.'

'Yes, Routley speaking, what is it, Phillips.' Clutching the receiver, the Inspector listened intently.

The voice at the other end of the line sounded animated. 'Sir, we've found it, the green van, in a remote country lane, some miles outside Nettlebridge Village.'

Inspector Routley's spirits lifted, things were looking up. 'And the driver?'

'He ...' The line went dead.

The Inspector rattled the cradle.

'I'm sorry, Sir ... I pulled out the wrong plug,' said the Operator. 'I'll try to connect you.' In the intermittent silence, the Inspector felt a mounting agitation.

A voice came back. 'Sir, there's still no reply.'

'Really Miss, I might have been on the point of making a breakthrough, in an investigation.' The Inspector remarked caustically, before slamming down the telephone receiver. He gave a deep sigh. Couldn't anyone be relied upon. The next moment, 'Yes,' he said briskly in response to a knock on the door. 'What is it?'

'Your coffee, Sir.'

'Take it away!' the Inspector exclaimed. Burying his head in his hands, he muttered, 'Doesn't anyone listen any more, I wanted tea.'

CHAPTER 15

'Another cup of coffee, dear?' The Vicar's wife peered over her half-rims.

'No thank you,' Ralph said abruptly, adjusting his dog-collar.

'You hardly ate anything at breakfast, I thought perhaps ...'

Ralph's eyes took on a far-away look. He got to his feet, crossed to the French windows and looked out onto the garden.

'Is something wrong?' Maria frowned. 'You're so quiet.'

'It's nothing really.'

Ralph, something is wrong, isn't it? Come here. Sit down and tell me all about it.' She pointed to an easy chair.

Ralph sank into it.

'Go on,' she coaxed, putting her hand on his shoulder.

Ralph stared at the carpet. 'What's the use?' He cupped his head in his hands.

'Darling, is it the gypsies?'

He looked up his eyes meeting those of his wife. 'It's just that I ... I feel so alienated.'

She raised a questioning eyebrow.

'The villagers, my congregation and particularly that Mildred Marsh.'

'Mildred Marsh?' Her eyes searched his face.

'There's something evil about that woman. Feelings are running high between the villagers and the gypsies.' He ran fingers through his thinning hair. He paused. 'I think she's behind it.'

'Stirring?' Maria frowned. 'Never! She's a regular churchgoer, isn't she?'

'Was a regular! I blame myself. I should have intervened when she was arguing with that gypsy in the church porch.' Ralph sighed. 'But I didn't. She puts the fear of God into me.' He smiled wryly at his pun. 'I must do something. I'll pay her a visit.'

'Don't let things get you down, Darling.' Maria smiled sweetly. On a lighter note she changed the topic. 'Julie's enjoying her holiday with the Guides; she's sent us a postcard. It's up there on the mantelpiece.' She reached up and handed it to him.

'That's nice.' Ralph mustered up a smile, scanned it, stood up and placed it back by the clock. 'I think I'll go for a short stroll, it will clear my head,' he said, his senses invigorated by the steady rotation of a mower, and a smell of newly mown grass wafting through the open French windows. Drawn to the sound and smell, he stepped outside.

A morning sun filtered through the branches of an ancient oak, it's leaves rustling in the breeze. Birds chirped in the thickets as he neared the gate, where over an old dry-stone wall a profusion of summer roses climbed in wild abandonment, petalled faces to the sun. Ralph, oblivious to such natural beauty, for within five minutes he would face Mildred Marsh. How would she react?

The village street was relatively quiet. The Blue Boar public house, once the life and soul of the community, particularly on Saturday nights was now almost deserted except for a few stragglers. The jolly ruddy face but now at times, doleful expression on the bartenders face spoke volumes. Whispers amongst villagers implied that given time with its closure, up would go a 'For Sale' sign. And who would want to buy it then?

The church hall had proved a poor supplement with it's slide shows, guest speakers, whist drives and bingo. There was talk that even the Flower Show in the vicarage grounds had been a disaster, with just a few entries, most of the villagers now taking the train or car to Chillingford, a nearby market town, in search of other pursuits. There had even been a decline in those attending Sunday Services.

Since the Nettleford village store had closed, the heart had gone out of the village. Due to the unexpected and mysterious disappearance of the Proprietor, Mr. George McDonald, the store once a hotbed for gossip, now like a morgue. Mindful of George's fastidiousness and attention to detail, Ralph averted his eyes as he strolled passed the grimy lifeless shop front.

Soon Mildred Marsh's cottage came into view, a melancholy Ralph somewhat surprised on his approach, to see the curtains drawn. Mildred had always been an early riser. He stood on the front doorstep and pressed the brass bell. Looking back at the well-kept garden, he wondered what he would say to her. There was no sound from within, no shuffling footsteps in the passage-way. He pressed the bell once more, raising the flap, he looked through the letter box but could only see part of a dim hallway. Perhaps she hadn't heard, had overslept. Why not try the back?

He knocked loudly on the back door but got no response. He lifted the latch finding to his surprise it opened. He called out, 'It's Ralph from the Vicarage, can I come in?' A heavy silence prevailed, tentatively, pushing open the door, he stepped into a low beamed kitchen.

There was no sign of Mildred. With everything in it's place, just a steady tick of the kitchen clock on the whitewashed wall. 'Where was she?' Not knowing what to think in the eerie si-lence, his heart pounding, he waited patiently. The clock ticked. He visualised Mildred with a rush of feet, threatening him with a carving knife. But the clock just ticked away. He shrugged his shoulders. Perhaps as Maria had implied it was all in his mind.

Somewhat disappointed at Mildred's non-appearance, he made his way up the narrow side path to the front door. Thwarted, his impetus now like a pricked balloon, he chided himself, for hav-ing steeled himself and achieved nothing.

Standing on the front step, he took out a notebook and pen-cilled, 'Called to see you, we've missed you at church, Ralph.' At least on her return, Mildred would know that he had paid her a visit, that he cared. Consoled by the thought, he pushed the slip of paper through the letterbox. It plopped down inside.

༄

CHAPTER 16

Bells punctuated the still night, bright beams lit up a weatherworn sign, as the ambulance, blue lights flashing bypassed the village of Nettlebridge.

Beyond the fields and hedgerows, the rosy glow of cottage lights went on intermittently, and not far away in the gypsy camp, squat around the flames of a roaring fire, shadowy figures, just back from a night's poaching, fell silent.

In a star spangled woodland, a tawny owl silently winged its way through a network of trees. Marco pricking up his ears, stopped in his tracks. His heart beating, he listened intently. There is was again, in the distance, an urgent summons, but now fainter.

In the moonlight, Marco black eyes widened, when fired by a thought. Oh no not Charlie! It can't be. He shouldn't have left him. But who could blame him. He felt tired and despondent, out at end. His legs covered in bruises and scratches ached. His hands stung with stinging nettles. His loose crimson tunic, torn and spattered with mud clung to his torso, his over trousers hanging baggily from his waist. Charlie was always lagging behind and holding him up. Even at that moment he felt a sense of irritation, just thinking about it. 'Charlie must learn our gypsy ways,' Marco muttered under his breath, 'and quickly too. But where is'e now, an' wot's 'e bin doin'?'

Marco leant against the trunk of a sturdy oak tree and pondered, shaken from his reverie, with a rabbit scuttling across the rough stony track in front of him, he chivvied himself. 'Marco, make up yer mind, can't 'e?' He silently mouthed. 'Go back to the encampment or retrace yer steps?' Wot I'd do to git me nashers into one of Ma's rabbit pies. The thought drove him on, but nagged by another, he stopped. What if Ma's in one of her moods, she'll want to know where he'd been. What he'd been doing?'

Still undecided, Marco carried on for a while in the same direction. Tired, he stopped to catch his breath. 'No!' He cried. 'Not even fer Ma's rabbit pie. I must find Charlie. I left 'im in the lurch. It will be me own fault if anythin' 'appens to 'im.' Marco thought of the last time, he'd seen Charlie crossing the field. Charlie had waved, he had waved back, but he hadn't wanted to wait. Charlie was so slow. I'll find me way to the village,' he told himself. 'An' see wot's goin' on.'

In the village, Marco with practised ease merged with the shadows, dodging into unlit alleyways, around corners on hearing voices or the echo of approaching footsteps. Systematically, he avoided the glare of street lights, lamp lit windows or the unexpected. Something really was up but why, where or how?

Further up the street, a circle of people were grouped outside the church gates, a hubbub of voices, but what were they talking about? He crept closer, taking refuge behind a Morris Minor parked conveniently nearby.

'No one really knows,' he heard one voice say, 'but Charlie Blackmore's not home yet and his Ma's frantic, has anyone seen him?' A comment followed by a brief negative silence. There was no sign of Charlie's Ma, although a short distance away, the old stone cottage was ablaze with lights.

'And where's Mildred Marsh?' Broke in another. 'No-one seen her for days, her curtains are drawn in the cottage. The Vicar said she doesn't answer the door at all when he calls. It's all very strange. Something's going on, I feel it in my bones, do you know what I mean?'

'Well if you want my opinion, I think them travellers are behind it, whatever it is. I blame Farmer Brown; he should never have let them have the field. Can't he find any other revenue, maybe campers, boy-scouts, you know decent people, why only yesterday ...'

'Now, now that quite enough, we're all God's creatures, we must think the best and help one another.' The Rev Ralph Watson, had joined the group.

'That's all very well, Vicar,' Mrs. Vera Vickery, a member of the church council and not one to be trifled with, remarked caustically, 'I'm not having my Jimmy mixing with those gypsies, you don't know where they've been.'

'I should say so,' said another, 'Give 'em an inch and they'll take a mile and then where will you be?'

A consensus of murmurs and mutters, the Vicar turned to go, now well aware that it was fruitless to intervene.

Marco intrigued by this unknown benefactor, moving furtively around the car to get a closer look, saw a man with a pleasant face. 'So that's the Vicar,' he muttered, ''im over there with the dog collar. That's wot 'e looks like. Charlie had mentioned him on several occasions, because he lived in the cottage across the road from the church he supposed. But no-one had listened to the Vicar, anymore than they would have listened to Mario.

Marco's tummy rumbled. With spots of rain, he would have to go home. He didn't want to, but he thought of Ma's rabbit pie. 'Perhaps there's some leftovers. I'll whip some when 'er back's turned, or when 'er's asleep.' He licked his lips, quite relishing the prospect.

The Vicar had disappeared and there was no sign of any ambulance, not that Marco had expected to see any. But where was Charlie? Still none the wiser, Marco slipped silently away into the night.

⚬⚬⚬

The patrol car nosed it's way through the maze of dark country lanes in the wake of the ambulance.

'Well I must say, this is really out in the sticks,' commented Constable Sidney Perkins, 'I havn't a clue where we are, have you?' He glanced sideways at his colleague, Constable James Harrison,who silent and unresponsive, kept his eyes fixed on the road ahead.

'Did you hear me, Jim, or shall I call you James,' Perkins remarked sarcastically, a teasing expression in his grey green eyes. His lips parting in a smile, smugly, he settled back cosily into the passenger seat.

'It alright for you, you just sit there.' Harrison responded, belligerently, picking up on his tone. 'Anyway, why do I always have to do all the driving, particularly in the dark, with all these twists and turns … By the way, how's the boy? He's very quiet.'

Perkins turned around in his seat to get a glimpse of the shadowy occupant in the back seat. 'Asleep, and the dog.'

Harrison yawned, momentarily losing concentration, he quickly corrected the patrol car, as it swerved, his dark eyes widening. 'I'm tired, I must be losing my beauty sleep.' He grimaced, 'Better watch what I'm doing.'

'Yeah, didn't expect this, my missus wasn't amused,' responded Perkins. He stretched and rubbed his eyes. 'We'd just turned out the light. Still this could be better than traffic control, don't you think? Once we get used to it.' He frowned. 'I wonder if it's what Routley got in mind for us permanent like, what do you think?'

'Dunno,' Harrison slowed down, as just ahead the ambulance, rounded a corner.

'Wherever are we?' Perkins wiped away the condensation obscuring his vision, from a side window, and peered out.

'Lor' only knows,' commented Harrison, 'I hope the ambulance driver knows where he's going.'

'Funny business, don't you think Jim?' Perkins sat back and mused. 'I mean the fellow in the van. At first I thought he was drunk, and then I thought, he's dead.'

Harrison now warming to the subject replied, 'Yes it is, apparently his names George McDonald, the village storekeeper, you know Nettlebridge, that village we've just passed where Phillips hangs out, Robbie Phillips, that raw recruit, whose just joined the Force. They'll be taking McDonald to the main hospital for observation.' He paused. 'But what about the boy?' Harrison glanced in the rear view mirror. His heart went out to the fair-haired boy curled up on the back seat with the dog sprawled beside him. The animal aware of his interest, raised his head, curled his lip and growled, then to Harrison's relief, in a sweeping motion, laid down and shut his eyes.

'Dunno,' replied Perkins. He struck a match and lit up a cigarette. 'All I could get out of the boy was "I wanna go 'ome an' where's Marco?"'

'Mmn … Marco, an odd name, unusual.' Harrison frowned. 'I hope he's not mixed up with the wrong crowd.' He sighed. 'Times are changing and not for the better and he's only a young lad.'

'Yes and look at the state he's in. He's covered in bruises, scratches, needs a good wash, and we haven't even got a blanket to put over him. Whatever could he have been up to at that time of night and with that mutt?' Perkins caste a disdainful glance at the sleeping dog. 'But the boy would come with us.' He stubbed out his cigarette, wiped the window and looked out. 'Still it's lighter now and it's stopped raining. Chillingford's coming into sight over them fields.' He indicated distant pin points of light twinkling in the grey landscape.

'Yes,' said Harrison, turning off the window wipers. 'I think you're right, we'll soon be there and then they'll see to the boy … and the dog.'

෴

CHAPTER 17

Constable Robbie Phillips standing in the dimly lit hallway, lifted his navy blue greatcoat from the hallstand. He glanced in the mirror, adjusted his black tie and flicked a hair off his coat. Then, as was his habit, he pulled back the curtains of a side window. The overnight rain had given way to a grey, crisp September morning.

He opened the door, stepped outside. A light wind rustled the autumnal leaves of a copper beech tree in the lane. Outside the gate parked by the kerb, propped on its stand, his Triumph motorcycle, it's chrome and forest green bodywork glistening with glimpses of the sun. A one-time budding mechanic, he had not long rescued the bike from a breakers yard.

Robbie checked his watch. Ten minutes to spare. He fished a packet of Senior Service from his pocket. For five minutes he would be at peace with the world.

Robbie drew on his cigarette and watched the smoke spiral. His mind switched back to the wide-eyed, panic stricken gypsy boy he had questioned on the night of the violent robbery at the Gables.

He had gasped, to tell you Mister Policeman … a murder at the big 'ouse.'

'Calm down, Son. What's your name? You're from the gypsy encampment, aren't you?'

'What if I am, Mister? I 'ain't done anythin' wrong, me and Charlie 'eard it.' The boy had fled into the night.

Robbie inhaled again, his line of thought broken by a formation of geese flying overhead. He glanced at his watch.

He recalled, the house to house enquiries in the village with a very disgruntled Inspector Routley, frustrated with useless information, false leads and unnecessary paperwork.

It was evident that there was no love lost between the villagers and the gypsies. But the green van with its shadowy occupant, located in a remote country lane, he had thought a break-through. Pity his subsequent call to the Inspector had finalised in a breakdown of communication.

'I want tidy ends with a result ... now.' Routley had stormed on many occasion, but last night it had been 'Mingle with the villagers, Phillips, win their confidence. Better still mingle with the gypsies, before things really get out of hand.'

Mingle with the gypsies, his presence would certainly arouse their suspicions, Robbie thought, but dare not voice an opinion. In his present state of mind, Routley was not to be trifled with.

The church clock struck the hour. He glanced at his wrist-watch, stubbed out his cigarette 'Time to go,' he muttered. From within, just as he turned to lock the front door, he heard the persistent summons of the telephone. Whoever's that, just as I'm going on duty too.'

Once inside the dark recesses of the hall, he picked up the receiver.

'Hello ... This is Nettleford Constabulary, Constable Rob-bie Phillips speaking.'

'Phillips, Routley here,' barked the familiar voice.

Robbie stiffened, immediately on guard. What did he want now? He wondered.

'Yes Sir?'

'We've located the green van in an isolated lane someway outside Nettleford.'

'I knew it had been found Sir. I rang and told you. But we got cut off.'

'Yes well ... there was a boy at the scene and in the vehicle a man. It appears that the occupant of the vehicle had taken an over-dose. There was a half a bottle of whisky lying at his feet, and an almost empty bottle of pills. The ambulance men resuscitated him and he should be in Chillingford Hospital right now, in recovery. Does that compare favourably with your version of events, Phillips?'

'Yes Sir, but what boy?' Somewhat puzzled, Robbie ques-tioned himself. He had been made aware of the man in the ve-hicle. But there had been no mention of a boy.

'A village boy, he's with Perkins and Harrison, I've taken them off Traffic Control. Apparently, the boy was in a state of shock, they couldn't get much out of him, only that he wanted to go home and where's Marco?' Marco, I wonder who this Marco is.' Mmn … We shall have to make further enquiries. Anyway, the boy refused point blank to go in the ambulance, but preferred the patrol car, and insisted on taking with him a rather scruffy dog.'

Where was all this leading to? Thought Robbie. 'But Sir, what do you want me to do?'

'Nothing Phillips, at the moment,' said the Inspector, 'Just keeping you up to scratch. Oh, incidentally, there was something … the Colonel. As you know, our investigations were suspended because of the coma. It seemed at one stage that the Colonel would never come out of it. You'll be glad to know, he's made a miraculous recovery. That's all for now.' The line went dead.

Robbie with misgivings replaced the receiver. 'So it is going to be a routine day after all,' he murmured, adding with hindsight, 'and probably a boring one. But come to think of it was Marco that panic stricken gypsy boy, and was it Charlie Blackmore, who had uttered when questioned, 'I want to go home and where's Marco?'

From upstairs, a voice broke the silence. 'Are you alright dear, I thought I heard voices?'

'Yes love, go back to sleep, it's early yet … see you tonight.' I wonder, thought Robbie as he made his way down the steps, two at a time. If today is going to be so boring after all.

⚬⚬⚬

CHAPTER 18

Iris Blackmore awakened from a troubled sleep, sat up in bed. She glanced at the luminous hands of her alarm clock. A cool breeze ruffled the flimsy curtains somewhere the wailing of a siren did nothing for her equilibrium.

The previous evening as darkness fell, with no sign of Charlie, she had phoned the village constabulary. Robbie Phillips had promised to put a call out. He said he would ring her if there was any news. Harry at the time, not in the least perturbed, had said. 'Don't jump the gun, wait and see, boys will be boys.'

Iris slipped out of bed and pulled on her candlewick dressing gown, her husband singularly unaware, still lying on his back, snoring. She grimaced. 'How could Harry sleep, when Charlie was missing?'

She shuffled across the lino in her well-worn slippers, her arthritic joints creaked as she made her way unsteadily down the stairs. At the hallstand mirror she paused, studied her reflection. The furrows on her forehead were deeper now. 'This will be the death of me,' she muttered. 'What's Charlie up to now? Where could he have got to? He's too young for girlfriends. Surely he wouldn't stay overnight at Billy's place without telling me.' Then a frightful thought entered her mind. She buried her head in her clammy hands. Her pulse raced. Was he out poaching with the gypsy boy, Marco? If so any moment, she'd expect to find the police on the doorstep.

In the kitchen, she tentatively pulled aside the net curtain and peered out, not a soul to be seen. The group of villagers by the church gates, who had come to take a personal interest or gloat now tucked up in their beds.

She reached for the kettle, lit the gas and placed it on the hob. Cupping a mug of black coffee laced with brandy, she sat down on the nearest chair. The hot liquid revitalised her. She

114

emptied the mug, rinsed it under the tap and pondered. What should she do now?

The steady tick of the wall clock constantly reminded her of the passage of time. Seated, she found herself needlessly glancing at her wristwatch. What if Charlie was lying somewhere badly injured or even dead? What if he was never found, had just disappeared off the face of the earth? Her mind in a whirl, she grasped the edge of the table and rose stiffly, on legs that didn't seem her own.

In a short space of time, clad in a skirt and blouse, she reached for her coat and hat. She glanced at the telephone willing it to ring. She stepped outside, locked the door and hurried up the path to the gate.

Heralding the dawn chorus, the darkness lightening, now gave way to a pearly grey sky, the reddish hues of a copper beech in the churchyard opposite shimmering in the early morning light.

For Iris now, time was at a premium. Soon the Constabulary on the edge of the village loomed into sight.

'I'm here at last.' She gasped, her breath visual on the morning air. On the topmost step, she paused, pressed the chrome bell. She heard footsteps from within. The door swung open. Melanie, Robbie's wife, her dark hair, dishevelled, stared at her.

'Can I speak to Robbie?'

'I'm afraid not, he's out, 'Melanie, pulled her dressing gown around her. 'Haven't you heard? A village boy's missing.'

'Yes, that's why I'm here …'

'Are you by any chance, the boy's mother, … Mrs. Blackmore?' Iris nodded.

'Then you really must be worried.' She smiled sympathetically. 'As soon as your sons found, you'll be the first to know. We've got your telephone number. But now I really must get dressed. By the way, before I do, did you hear an ambulance at some unearthy hour this morning?'

'Sort of,' said Iris. 'When I was trying to get some sleep. I hope it's not my Charlie.'

'I should think, it was on it's way to Chillingford Hospital, if that's any help.'

'Well you never know, there may be a connection,' said Iris feebly. 'Any port in a storm, I suppose.' Low in spirits, she mustered up a smile and turned to go. 'Thanks anyway.'

Iris caught the first available bus to Chillingford, by now convinced that this was her only option. On her arrival in the forecourt of the hospital, she saw a number of ambulances, but no police cars, but just outside the entrance a news vendor, huddled up on the steps, against a nippy, crisp, September morning.

As she neared, he caught sight of her, and tipped his cap. 'Paper, Missus, read all about it. Green van located in remote country lane. Case reopened.' Iris reached out and handed him some coins. He gave a toothless smile. She found a wrought iron seat nearby, on which she sat and perused the newspaper. Although not a good likeness, she deduced there was no doubt about it, the boy in the caption must be Charlie.

She walked briskly through the gates and down the road, in the direction of the police station. Not sure, only a stone's throw away from the entrance, on a grassy verge, she hesitated. Suppose Charlie had got in with the wrong company, and when questioned liable to give the wrong impression, so easily led, it could make things worse. As to the ambulance, time would tell. Had she not better try to find him herself and bring him home with a flea in his ear?

❧

The sun high in the sky, Charlie mid afternoon, with Rover at his heels found his way home. Ma out, the cottage empty as he had known it would be, it being market day in Chillingford, she would have caught the train and with Dad at work wouldn't be home until teatime.

He hadn't wanted to go home in the first place, but had had no choice. Hungry tired, and dirty, he had had enough. He told the two coppers that he wanted to find Marco, but his words having fallen on stony ground, so when an opportunity had arisen, he had given them the slip. Upstairs in his room, Charlie covered in grim lay down on his bed to think things over. A thought occurred. Wasn't it through Marco that he was always in disgrace? Some friend, he'd turned out to be making off. He shuddered to think what sort of mood Ma would be in when she came home to find him back at last and in such a state. He would have to douse himself and the dog with water from the pump in the backyard. Ma was right, she was had told him not to mix with travellers, then wasn't Ma always right. But how boring life would be without any fun. His mouth dry, his stomach rumbled. At least there was plenty of food and drink in the larder, he'd take his pick. A dark thought occurred. But what if there wasn't any, it being market day.

⁂

The journey in the ambulance had not been an easy one for George McDonald, laying on a stretcher under the watchful eye of the nurse, he thought, I should be dead. With so much discomfort, as the vehicle jerked and bumped over ruts and dips in the road, his mind as active as ever, haunted by the face at the window, he had become constantly aware of being very much alive. The image, his first conscious impression of the real world around him, the world he had tried so hard to escape, a harsh reality, mirrored in the expression on the boy's face. The son he would never really get to know as a father, who through a cruel twist of fate would never recognise him as one. What lay ahead? Who could tell?

He shuddered inwardly, with a vision of Mildred Marsh as she bent over the Colonel, with evil intent, her face contorted, her ears deafened to the old man's pleas for mercy. A respected storekeeper, he had succumbed to her threats and inadvertently become involved in a violent robbery. Panic stricken, he had fled the scene. Now, like a snake if threatened, Mildred would recoil and strike, and reveal all, that is her version of the story. The game was up.

In no time, George, as if in a dream, found himself in a world of lighted corridors, with muted voices and smiling faces. In an

117

atmosphere, with a strong smell of disinfectant, in which white coated images passed through doors that constantly opened and closed, a place where his mind switched off, not wanting to take in the gravity of the situation.

'There, there you get some sleep now.' Was it the voice of an angel, so soft and gentle, so caring and different from that of his mother and Mildred Marsh. Was the voice really speaking to him? By now George completely disorientated, had closed his eyes, and drifted off into a deep sleep.

CHAPTER 19

An autumnal nip in the air signified the end of one season and heralded the next. Mario felt the old wanderlust in his bones, that of another place, beyond the far horizon. He stood on the topmost step of the caravan, his very being in tune with the raucous cries of rooks in the clear air, the twitter of birds in hedgerows and copses, bordering pathways now carpeted with leaves of red and gold.

'The sun's lost it's strength,' he muttered, buttoning up his embroidered waistcoat. He shivered. 'Time to move on, but where?'

He was about to answer his own question when he heard the crunch of boots.

'Talkin' to yerself, first signs.' Lorenzo, a drinking buddy of Mario's glanced up, his good natured face crumbled into a smile.

'Up an' 'bout already, 'ows that?' Mario raised an eyebrow.

'Bin over to look at the 'orse, 'e ain't 'appy. I shall 'ave to shoe 'im before 'e goes lame.' Lorenzo having lit a fire with a pile of dead sticks and torn up boxes, crouched over it waiting for the kettle to boil.

'I was thinkin' …' Mario said philosophically. He didn't finish his sentence for a V formation of geese flew overhead, honking over the treetops, to disappear beyond the skyline. 'See wot I mean, they knows wot's best fer 'em?' He grimaced. 'The cold weather, I feels it in me bones.'

'T'is time fer a meetin', I suppose,' said Lorenzo, warming his hands. 'W'ose goin' to call it? Suppose 'e wants me to. On second thoughts, it's your turn.'

'Me?' Mario pursed his lips. 'Leonardo's always grousin' when the cold bites, why can't 'e? 'e gits on Meg's nerves, 'an 'er wi all them kiddies too, it ain't fair. Come to think of it I 'aven't seen 'im 'round for a bit. Glad me own's grown up an' left 'ome 'cept Marco, aren't 'e yourn?'

'Got any ideas, of yer own, 'bout movin on?' Lorenzo asked, determined not to be sidetracked.

'Nothin' to speak of but if us is stuck Salvatore will come up wi' somethin'. That's if 'e ain't out fishin' like last time and Chianti wi all her bairns ain't in one of 'er moods.' Mario took of his cap and scratched his head. 'Anyway, us gypsies generally puts it to the vote. Tonight then, seven o'clock 'ere on the dot.'

'ere?'

Mario nodded. 'Where else. That's if it ain't rainin' us'll set match to a fire.'

'A crate of ale will loosen their tongues, that'll git the meetin' goin' Pass the word 'round. Let's 'ope they all turn up. Giorgio will fer the ale.' Lorenzo stretched, and yawned. 'Talk of the devil ...'

'That's me.' Giorgio sidling up plonked down in-front of them. A seedy bearded character, cunning without any scruples, always keeping an ear to the ground, he laid down a bucket brimful of water. 'Bin up to the pump, thought I'd best show willin' 'er's bin complainin', says I's lazy.'

'Well ain't 'e? Thought e'd gone fishin', can't see any, 'ows that?' Mario wrinkled his brow.

'Got sidetracked, wos in the Blue Boar. Didna stay long, got thrown out.' Giorgio's s eyes danced with mischief, his thick lips parting revealed a single gold tooth. 'Don' 'e tell the Missus. 'Er be thinkin' the fish 'adn't bin tempted.' A shrewd pair of dark eyes viewed them from under the brim of a well worn trilby. 'Best be goin' ... what's this 'bout ale?'

'A meeting, you'm invited. Be 'ere tonight seven o'clock sharp.' Mario drew out and relit his clay pipe.

'fer the ale, or the meetin? Don' 'e' answer that.' Giorgio with a cheeky grin on his face, picked up the bucket and whistling, went on his way.

'Tried out the shotgun yet?' asked Lorenzo, his eyes fixed first on his receding figure and then on the weapon, propped against Mario's caravan, where Mario had left it.

Mario clutching a large mug of sweetened tea, had hoped he would raise the subject. And now he had. It was days ago he had exchanged a harness for the double-barrelled shotgun. He would put it through its paces later on.

'Ah, 'ere's Bianca with the pan, 'er will be makin' breakfast. 'Er'll be fryin' eggs and bacon.' Lorenzo gulped his tea. 'ave 'e fed them banties of yourn, last time I sees 'em me thought them poor birds ain't got long to go.'

'Still eatin' off that battered old tin plate, are 'e?' Mario couldn't resist taking a dig.

Lorenzo sat on an upturned bucket, savouring the aroma, ignored the jibe.

'Get that down 'e.' Bianca her face glowing with heat, handed him the plate.

'I've bagged a few pheasies in me time,' he said between mouthfuls,' with that old shotgun, 'aven' t I, Bianca?'

'You'm jokin, 'usband' She flashed her white teeth. 'ave 'e checked them traps 'e set?'

'Nope.' Lorenzo, shrugged his shoulders. 'Should I 'ave?'

'If 'e wants to eat.' Bright eyed, straddled legged, Bianca her shining black hair, unbraided, hitched up her muslin skirt and squat down beside him.

'I wos 'oping to bag a rabbit like last time.' Lorenzo rubbed his greasy hands on a rag.

Watching them, Mario smacked his lips when thinking of Eliza's rabbit pies straight from the oven, his mouth watered, his stomach rumbled at the thought. Talkin' of food, I'm 'ungry. See 'e at suppertime.' He drained his mug.

Back in the wagon, Mario found a sizable piece of cheese. T'will do for me breakfast, he thought, buttering a hunk of crusty bread, he ate heartily. Eliza sound asleep, oblivious, in her cot Juanita hadn't stirred.

There was little sign of life from the huddle of caravans, except for Leonardo, bent double, repairing a wagon wheel. Dour faced, he stood up when catching sight of Mario.

'Mawnun, 'ows Meg?' Mario hollered.

'er's alright, 'er's out wi' the trap, 'oping to pick up a thing or two. Childes at school if of a mind, 'ave to take 'em away when us moves on.'

'Us be 'oldin' a meeting 'bout seven tonight 'round me fire, 'bout movin' on. Comin'? Lorenzo, me neighbours comin' Giorgio's comin an' Salvatore, that if Chianti wi'all 'er brood ain't in one of 'er moods.

'A bit cold fer that ain't it?' Leonardo at the thought, pulled his shabby overcoat around him.

'I'll set the fire ablazin' an' there'll be plenty of ale.'

'Suppose I ought to.'

'Suppose you 'ad, else us could leave 'e behind, if that's wot 'e wants' Mario chuckled. A mischievous look in his eyes, shouldering his shotgun, he crunched through the frosty grass towards the five-bar gate where met by a pack of yelping stray dogs, he spotted an inimitable Jack Russell. His eyes brightened. By virtue of its size and fearless nature he admired the rough haired terrier he had christened Amigo.

Amigo wasted little time in taking advantage of his privileged position. Mario bent and lovingly ruffled the dog's silky pointed ears.

Like Mario, the rough-haired terrier was beset with a wanderlust. Often he disappeared from the encampment for days, but to Mario's relief, eventually returned in search of food.

Mario closed the gate and headed up a rutted unofficial footpath towards the edge of a deciduous woodland. By a beech hedge he stopped, distracted by an unusual sound. He cocked his ear. What was it?

The gypsy became aware of a movement in the undergrowth. He froze. The next moment he spotted a feral cat, a bird in its mouth. The cat hadn't seen him. It kept padding stealthily towards him. Mario levelled the shot gun. The creature detected his movement. It stopped, dropped its prey.

Should he fire? The creature fixed its eyes on him. He didn't know why, but he pressed the trigger. The shot rang out, echoed among the tall trees. He felt a rush of adrenaline. The cat's eyes widened. It let out a deep-throated snarl, and leapt into the undergrowth.

Mario was filled with remorse. He could feel his pulse racing, blood surging through his veins. Had he killed the feral cat, or injured, was it laying on the grass in its death throes, its intestines spilling out? He recoiled at the horror of it.

'Mario, Mario, where's 'e gone! Eliza's strident voice carried, setting off the dogs, the noise drawing a number of gypsies from out of their wagons.

Mario sighed. 'Wot now?' He parted the foliage with his hand and peeped out. Eliza stood in the field, glancing this way and that with a tearful Juanita, clutching her billowing skirts.

'There 'e is, a woman shouted. 'Over there.' It was Bianca who pointed towards the copse.

'Our Marcos scarpered, I can't fin' 'im anywhere!' Eliza's face was drawn, her breath coming out in gasps, as Mario drew abreast. 'I's all aches 'an pains, 'e promised 'e wouldn.'

'Promises, 'e'd promise 'e anythin' Mother.'

'Wot!' Eliza's voice rose, she stared at Mario, there was a dangerous look in her eyes.

Mario squirmed. 'Nothin', Liza ...' He searched for words. 'Wi'out 'im, t'is nice an' quiet, don' 'e think?'

'Quiet, quiet,' Eliza shrieked. 'Do 'e 'onestly call theese quiet? 'e don't care a fig fer 'es ole mother and wot 'er' be thinkin.' With arms akimbo Eliza glanced around, at an amused and embarrassed assembly. 'I've 'nough wi Juanita.' She pointed an accusing finger at the little girl, who as if on cue, let out another wail.

'There, there Mother don' 'e take on so.' Mario felt a modicum of pity. He patted her on the shoulder. 'Don' 'e worry, Marco's a young lad, 'e can't keep 'im cooped up, can 'e? I'll find 'im, 'e see to 'er.'

Mario watched as a disgruntled Eliza accompanied by Bianca, with a tearful Juanita in tow, made her way back to the wagon.

There was an awkward silence, as Mario turned to go, a muted cheer. With Eliza gone, the mask slipped revealing a face wreathed in smiles, the gypsy took off his cap and bowed in response. And catching a glimpse of Lorenzo, Mario with a smirk on his face when their eyes met, winked.

Annoyed and humiliated, Mario set out once again.

In the sanctuary of the woods, Mario stopped to wipe his brow and collect his thoughts. 'Women,' he muttered, 'e' can't live with em', 'e can't live wi'out 'em.' He gave a drawn out sigh.

The gypsy's heavy heart grew lighter as he trod deeper into the wood. Now at home, he trudged along paths half hidden by falling leaves, in a timeless world. Now and again he paused to look around, aware of a rich kaleidoscope of colour. A dying scene, soon to be deprived of its beauty.

Startled by a rustle of leaves, he caught a glimpse of a creature. It wasn't a rabbit, maybe a fox. The fact that it had alluded him, frustrated Mario. On impulse, he looked along the barrel of his gun, aimed and fired in the animal's direction. He fired a second round, the bullet ricocheted, a strange cry emanating from within, one he had heard before. He approached the spot and prodded the dense undergrowth with a stick.

The feral cat, lay where it had died. Mario knelt down beside it. Although conditioned by an outdoor life, he felt only remorse. Covering the bloodstained body with leaves and foliage, he turned away, with mixed emotions. He thought of the mottled grey dog peppered with shots. Of Charlie, the village boy, of his distress and concern for the animal. Had the memory evoked finer feelings, feelings he would have once considered a weakness. Mildred what's her name had hardened his heart, but Charlie had set him thinking.

'Am I losin' me grip?' He mumbled. 'The cat mean't no 'arm. But where's me boy an' 'ow an' when will I fin' 'im. Soon I 'ope!

❧

CHAPTER 20

It was nearly midday when Marco stopping to rest beneath the branches of a spreading chestnut tree, would encounter the dog for the first time. At that moment, he had had no intention of returning to the gypsy encampment. For this break for freedom would hopefully, turn into an adventure, and one that he sorely needed. Maybe he'd even meet up with Charlie and when in his company accept him with all his faults.

He had just taken a bite of Ma's rabbit pie, surreptitiously smuggled into a threadbare haversack earlier that morning, and sipped some cold tea from that left overnight in the teapot, when it appeared. The sound of frantic barking heralded it's arrival as appearing as if from nowhere, the dog streaked past him.

Judging by it's colour and form, Marco had had a fleeting impression of a large dog, maybe an Alsatian. He watched as barking it bound in the direction of a steep embankment at the far end of the field, over which it vanished from sight.

'Dexter … Come back!' Although a command, the voice that rang out across the field was charged with uncertainty. Marco looking over his shoulder, saw a man making his way purposely in his direction.

'Boy, have you seen an Alsatian?' Out of breath, the ruddy faced man standing a few paces away, mopped his brow with a large cotton handkerchief.

Marco took another bite of the pie, finding it delicious even when washed down with cold tea from a flask.

'Well have you, or haven't you?' The stranger blustered, agitated by Marco's complacency.

Why should I tell 'im anythin', Marco thought. 'e ain't goin' to bully me, cos. I'm a gypsy.'

'Did you hear what I said?' The voice persisted.

'Suppose I did, wot of it,' Marco commented, then rather begrudgingly, 'If I did, 'e made off over there.'

'When I find that animal, t'will be a one way ticket to the Dog's Home, whatever the wife says,' the man muttered, scanning the direction in which Marco had pointed.

Marco watched him disappear over the ridge. Getting up he shouldered, his haversack, thinking he would go in the opposite direction, so their paths wouldn't cross.

So their paths weren't to cross, where they? He should be so lucky. Marco hadn't gone far when once again the familiar voice rang out across the sunlit field. 'Boy, where are you? I need your help.'

So wot, I ain't goin' to 'elp 'im, was Marco's immediate reaction. I'll make out I didn' 'ear.

Standing on the grassy embankment, Marco looking down, saw a sight on the railway line, that took his breath away. Below on the track he spotted not only the dog, but what looked like a body, the recalcitrant Alsatian standing guard.

Well, Marco thought, he'd wanted an adventure, hadn't he? Confused and uncertain, he scrambled down the bank, not knowing what to expect. Was it a body? Apprehensive, he shivered. Should he take a look? The dog was becoming restless. Had he picked up a scent, the smell of a human? Was it that of his owner? Something told Marco he shouldn't hang around. He looked up and down the railway track. Suppose he a gypsy if seen with the body, be accused of a violent assault? The dog's owner hadn't liked his offhand attitude. His 'I don' want to git involved' attitude may have in itself aroused the man suspicions Set him wondering, why was he, Marco a gypsy lingering in such a lonely place. With these thoughts, Marco verging on flight, scanned the railway track.

'Dexter!' an all too familiar panic stricken voice rang out. A figure emerged on the skyline. 'Ah, there you are, Boy. Wait there!'

Access to the line was easy for a part of the fence further down had sagged in the middle. Man and gypsy scrambling over, in their urgency, half running, half walking towards the body.

On their approach, the man managed a smile, because of this appearing not so hostile and far more approachable. His expression changing to one of shock when seeing the body. Silently, he stood and looked down at it. He knelt down to a take a detailed look. Marco keeping a wary eye on the dog, stood someway away. What was he thinking, he thought. What would he say?

After a while, the man stood up. 'I'll need your help.' Something about the tone of his voice, a urgency tinged with fear, persuaded Marco to stop, listen and consider. 'I've given her the kiss of life, but to no avail. You'd better stay here and keep an eye on Dexter, while I go for help. Don't worry you'll be quite safe, I won't be long.'

Marco wasn't convinced. He watched the retreating figure, with unthinkable thoughts. He didn't feel safe. What if the man reported him to the police, should he escape now while the goings good? But why? He hadn't done anything. But the murder at the big house. That's if it was a murder. Suppose the village copper spills the beans. He, Marco had panicked on the night of the robbery. He shouldn't have gone to the Police House.

But the woman what does she look like? Tentatively, Marco took a look. Appalled at the sight of a mangled body, he drew back and vomited on the spot. The Alsatian monitoring his movements, shifted his position and growled. Unabashed Marco made clicking noises.

Intrigued Marco mustering up courage, knelt to get a closer look. The woman by the way she was dressed, although mutilated beyond all recognition seemed vaguely familiar. A felt hat tilted at an angle, covered her face. With grubby fingers he lifted the brim, gasping at what he saw, the Alsatian whining in reaction. There in repose, her eyes shut, he saw the bloodied face of Mildred Marsh. Pale and unlined like one of Juanita's wax dolls, so different from that of the steely eyed, rosy cheeked face, he remembered seeing, when out and about in the village.

There was congealed blood on one of her gloved hands and on the handle of a leather handbag lying by her side. Nearby a bunch of trampled violets wrapped in tissue paper. In the shadows on the far side of the railway track, a suitcase with its contents spilling out.

Marco felt a sense of revulsion. He had never seen a dead person before but known instinctively that she was by the pallor of her face and the rigidity of her body. The Alsatian picking up on his demeanour, started to whimper and then bark.

'Quiet! Marco exclaimed. 'Quiet!' His cries, echoing along the track. He was beginning to wish he hadn't become involved, for any moment someone may appear and ask him what he was doing there.

Dexter pricked up his ears, his body stiffened, his amber eyes focused down the line. Nose to the ground, picking up a scent, the Alsatian started to wander, breaking into a run, at the sound of distant voices.

At that moment, the sun coming out from behind a cloud, caste a different perspective for Marco, eliminating a sudden sense of panic as far down the line etched against the distant horizon, dark silhouettes emerged. He eyed them with relief, a relief soon to be dispelled with doubts. The Police? What if they should recognise him and link him with the robbery at the Gables. Mario had said on many an occasion, 'Remember Son, it ain't good to be in the wrong place at the wrong time.' Whatever that meant. Anyway 'e an' Charlie 'adn't don' anythin', 'ad they? So with renewed confidence and a certain amount of pride, his head held high, Marco watched the figures gradually approach.

❧

As they neared the figures took shape, that of two men carrying a stretcher and three others, one of whom carried a black bag. The group of five were followed by Dexter and his owner.

Marco stood beside the inert body as the group approached. At first he felt at ease, that is, until he saw two officers of the law.

The party arrived, gasping for breath. The body having been examined and pronounced dead, the men from the ambulance set to work immediately, while one of the police officers, a man with an aquiline nose and bushy eyebrows, took a note book from a tunic pocket and started writing. The second walked off to a line side telephone.

Next, to Marco's surprise, Dexter bounded up and greeted him like a long lost friend.

'Good Boy.' Marco reacted spontaneously to the dog's enthusiasm, ruffling his ears.

His master arrived, sweat dripping from his face. 'You're still here,' he gasped, patting him on the shoulder.

Marco warmed to the stranger. 'Can I go now Mister?' He asked.

The policeman taking notes overheard his question. 'You stay where you are, Sonny, I shall want to take a statement.'

A dark thought occurred. Had the man suspected and reported him? His expression gave nothing away. Marco felt a sweat line creeping down his brow. And, what if the police connected him with the 'Gables? They were from the local force. They may even have been involved in the original investigations.

'I ain't done anythin', Mister. That man,' he pointed to the stranger and his dog, 'asked me to 'elp 'im.'

'Just routine Son.' The policeman gave a disarming smile. 'Nothing to worry about. You're from the gypsy encampment aren't you?'

Marco detected a certain suspicion in the Constable's words. Suddenly, he became aware of his muddy tunic and ragged trousers. He felt vulnerable. 'So wot if I is?'

The officer raised an eyebrow.

Marco flashed his dark eyes defiantly. ''Tis nothin' to do wi me, I ain't don' anythin'.'

'I'm not saying you have Son, but you were at the scene,' the policeman said matter-of-factly. 'What were you doing in the minutes before the body was discovered?'

Marco searched for words.

'Take your time, Son.'

Step by step Marco accounted for his movements, of his chance meeting with the stranger and his dog in the field, of his first sighting of the body on the line. Then he fell silent. 'That's all, Mister.'

'Well Son, that wasn't so bad was it?' Asked the constable, replacing his notebook. 'I may need to see you again.'

Marco relaxed, the tension drained from his body. 'Mister, there wos somethin.'

'Yes, go on Son.' The constable was all ears.

'Violets, a bunch, wrapped in paper. Them's by the body.' Having said that, without a backward glance, Marco having found the sagging fence, scrambled over, then up and over the cutting. He vaguely heard the policeman's shout, 'Take the correct walking route,' for once over the top, he had disappeared into the woods.

'There will have to be a post-mortem to establish the cause of death,' commented the doctor at that moment, in passing.

'Did you by any chance see any violets near the body?'

'Yes, as a matter of fact ... why?' came the reply.

'Oh nothing really, it's just ...' The constable having broken off the conversation, was now visualising the earnest expression on the gypsy boys face, when uttering the words, 'There wos somethin', violets, a bunch, wrapped in paper. Them's by the body.' Had the boy in some way been involved in the incident? Had, the verbal account of his movements leading up to the discovery of the body been merely a fabrication? He had had certainly seemed very much on the defensive and at times quite vague in his estimation, and extremely eager to go. What had he to hide?

He glanced around at a deserted branch line, cordoned off, now a peaceful scene with glimpses of the sun and elongated shadows. 'I wonder what really happened here', he mumbled.

The constable bent and picked up the bunch of violets. They had lain within arm's length from the body, indicating that the victim may have been holding them just before she died. Drooping, devoid of their beauty, the posy, still in its paper wrapper now crumpled and torn, tied with string had been in danger of being annihilated altogether, with the passage of so many feet. Baffled by the significance of the find, the constable untying the string was surprised to find inside a note on which was written 'To whom it may concern.' Unfolding it he read the following written in neat block capitals, 'I WISH IT TO BE KNOWN

THAT I WAS THE SOLE PERPETRATOR OF THE CRIME COMMITTED AT THE GABLES.' Below although spidery, a signature, one he made out to be that of a Mildred Marsh.

Mmn, mused the constable, The Gables, that name rings a bell. Surely that case over Nettlebridge way, the unsolved one that was shelved through lack of evidence. The one that 'Charlie' Routley was going on about. If so, what a turn up for the books. They'll never get over this back at the station, will they?

∽℘℘

CHAPTER 21

George McDonald awoke with a start. Where was he? Realization dawned as from the confines of a comfortable hospital bed now with the grey light of dawn filtering under the curtains, he recalled the previous day's events. An awareness of the discomfort of a bumpy ride in the ambulance came flooding back. A painful ride that had told him that he was truly alive, that his attempt to end it all had not worked. A feeling of remorse, one of failure encompassed him. But one thing stuck in his mind, that of the face of the boy at the side window. Slumped there in the van in his comatose state,was the image just a figment of his imagination, or there in reality? Was it his son? It had become an obsession, a living nightmare. To think the boy's last impression of him would have been that of a failure. Because of this and maybe this fact alone, no-one must ever know his true identity, that of the boy's father. A tap on the door interrupted this train of thought, prompting him to say automatically, 'Come in.' The door opened revealing that of a nurse carrying a breakfast tray.

'How are we this morning?' she enquired with a smile, placing the tray on a side table.

'Better,' he replied lamely, whilst she fussed around him, plumping up pillows, rearranging the bedcovers and drawing back the curtains. 'When will I be discharged, nurse?'

'All in good time,' she said, placing the tray in front of him. 'Now eat up. You've got to get your strength up, do you hear?'

Alone again, George propped up in bed, eyed the food disdainfully. This was not what he had in mind. The thought of going on hunger strike now didn't appeal, for the impetus, once so strong to end it all was now non-existent. Drained of any emotion and unable to resist, he emptied the plate in no time.

Through the window pane, shafts of morning sunlight lit up the austere hospital room, lightening his mood. A light breeze toyed with the curtains. Through the open window a sound of voices and activity in the courtyard below, reached his ears. Sustained by the food and lulled by the warmth and sanctuary of the bed he began to feel drowsy.

'Mr McDonald … George, are you awake?'

The voice seemed a long way away as if he was in another world, which he was at the time. A dream one of colonels, gypsies, a darkened shop in which a vindictive woman stood, there in the shadows creating a feeling in him of fear and inadequacy. Her voice cold and uncompromising, 'I will reveal your secret. I'll spread the word, just think in a village like Nettlebridge where everyone knows you, and you the storekeeper too. She cackled. 'But I won't that's if you …'

'Mr McDonald … George.' The timbre changed.

George perspiring and clammy, awoke with a start.

'Mr McDonald, are you alright?'

'Yes,' he replied, coming to his senses. He managed a smile, for once glad to be back in the living. 'Yes Nurse, quite alright.' But was he? Where was Mildred Marsh now, what was she saying and to whom? With the thought, he shivered, as if a shadow had temporarily darkened the sunlit room.

'I'm glad to hear it,' said the Nurse. 'Sit up, here, lean forward and let me straighten your pillows, that's it … better? My aren't you restless, the bedclothes are rumpled. Been having a nightmare? Anyway you have a visitor.'

Outside in the corridor, the bespectacled Ralph Watson had just sat down with the intention of reading a magazine. For some reason, he had not been relishing the prospect of a visit.

'Here,' his wife had said, earlier that morning when walking with him to the garden gate, 'take these.' She picked some flowers from the border and handed them to him. 'They're bound to cheer him up.'

But the Vicar wasn't so sure. The moment he stepped off the bus outside the hospital, he had bought a newspaper in the forecourt, thinking that it would take his mind of things. But it wasn't to be. At first he couldn't grasp the headlines or the spread on the front page. For there a familiar face looked back at him, above it in bold black type, 'Body Found On Line.' He read on. "The body of a middle-aged woman has been found on a railway line a few miles from the village of Nettlebridge. Mrs. Mildred Marsh, a widow and keen churchgoer had been missing for several days.'

Mrs Mildred Marsh, his Mrs Marsh? Although shocked and astounded, totally absorbed the Rev Ralph Watson read on.

'You can go in now, Vicar.' A voice followed by a discreet cough reiterated 'Rev. Watson, you can go in.'

'Oh! Sorry, thanks nurse,' he replied fixing her with an apologetic smile.

∽≗≗∽

George McDonald had never darkened the church door, so was pleased when after a time, the Vicar glancing at his wrist watch, got up to go, with the comment, 'Sorry, it's been such a flying visit, parish affairs you know, meetings and all that to attend, but I'll come again.'

George breathed a sigh of relief as the door closed behind him; he could do without the platitudes. But at least he had gained something for the Vicar had left his paper behind; it was lying folded on the bedside table.

He hungrily surveyed it.

'I'm surprised but glad to see you're taking an interest, Mr. McDonald.'

George looked up, currently lost for words when seeing the bemused expression on the nurse's face. Collecting his thoughts, he commented. 'It's you Nurse, I didn't know you were there.' He pointed to the photograph and the caption that had so enthralled the Vicar. 'The poor woman,' he commented with mock sincerity,' 'I wonder what drives people to such lengths.'

'Now there's no point in worrying about things you can do nothing about.' The nurse taking the paper away from him, folded it. 'Between you and me the doctors are very pleased, you'll soon be discharged. You're luckier than some. Don't do such a silly thing again; you might not be so lucky next time.'

'But Nurse …'

'I must go,' said the nurse brusquely, glancing at her fob watch. 'I've other patients to attend to. Try to get some rest while you have the chance.'

She made for the door.

Outside in the corridor, as the door swung open, a swarthy gypsy boy raised his head from the magazine he'd been purporting to read. Of no significant, the nurse barely noticed him. She hurried down the corridor, at the far end passing through swing doors.

Marco nervously glanced this way and that to make sure the coast was clear. By the door, he turned the handle.

♋

CHAPTER 22

I knew no good would come of it, I told you so.' Iris standing by the hob poked impatiently at the bacon sizzling in the pan. 'Smells good,' commented Harry, aware that she was in one of her moods and not to be trifled with.

'At least put the kettle on,' she retorted. 'Don't just sit there watching me.'

'I wasn't.' Harry sighed. He got up and folding the newspaper he had been reading, plugged in the kettle.

'Anything worth reading?' asked Iris.

'Nothing much but for a body found on a branch line, some woman or other.'

'Call that nothing! Give me the paper, and take this.' She handed him the spatula. 'And see it doesn't stick.'

Iris glanced at the front spread and it's caption. Her eyes widened, she gasped. 'Really Harry, nothing much. Is there something wrong with your eyesight? Don't you recognise her? So this explains her prolonged absence, I might have known.'

'Mildred Marsh?'

'Who else?' Iris firmed her lips. 'Really, Harry, sometimes I wonder if you're in the land of the living. I despair, why bother, that's what I tell myself, is it worth it?'

'It's sad isn't it?' Harry searched for words.

'Sad, sad …!' cried Iris, her eyes wild and expressive, her voice rising to a crescendo. 'You really think so. She was a horrible, horrible woman and now she's got her comeuppance.'

Harry surprised by such an unexpected outburst at first remained silent, then quietly and solemnly said. 'Iris, that's not very Christian-like.'

'I don't feel very compassionate about the likes of her,' Iris retorted, eyeing him disdainfully. 'And what about George Mc-Donald, where's he gone that's what I'd like to know. The village is going to pot, with no store.' She gave him a baleful look. 'You wouldn't know, you don't get around like I do, everyone's complaining without any basic food supplies, they have to journey into Chillingford. I don't like the veg in that new supermarket, amongst other things, it's mass produced. George could have warned us and not made off without any explanation.'

'Don't go on about it, dear,' said Harry cracking eggs into the pan. 'You can't do anything about it, and the bacons getting cold.'

'Didn't you put it in the oven to keep warm?'

Harry shook his head.

'I knew I should have done it myself.' Iris fumed.

I was right, Harold told himself. She is in a right mood.

At the table between mouthfuls, Iris gave vent to her wrath. 'And poor Emily, the poor soul with no car. We must give her a lift when next we go to Chillingford.' She got up and looked out the window. 'By the way, first thing this morning when I was out in the garden watering the plants, I spotted the Vicar. He was standing at the bus stop, holding a bunch of flowers. It's not like him. Who were they for I wonder?' Iris for a while, stared into space. The first to break the silence, she commented. 'Isn't the kettle boiling yet, Harry?' She glanced in it's direction. 'You know a watched kettle never boils.'

⌘

On hearing the click of the gate, the Vicar's wife, hands on knees in the process of trying to extract another stubborn weed from a profusion, looked up. She smiled on seeing her husband's satisfied expression and struggling to get up, clutched the side of her waist. 'My, I'm not so young as I was, and I've hardly made any inroads. See ...' She pointed to the wide expanse of lawn, to the ivy everywhere on the walls, around the trees. 'The builder told me to get rid of it, but it's easier said than done when it gets a grip. Anyway, that's enough about me, what about you, you look pleased.'

'In a way, I suppose I am.' Ralph closed the gate. 'But it was only a flying visit, I said I had other people to see.'

'You made an appearance, that's all that matters. How did he look?'

'Just like George always does, but at times he seemed confused. I expect it's only to be expected.'

'Did he seem pleased to see you?'

'I don't really know, he smiled when I got up to leave. I didn't know what to make of that.'

'Did you give him the flowers?'

'Yes, but he wasn't all that interested, he hardly looked at them. I bought a daily paper then left it behind. I hadn't even read it, but the headlines. Something about a body on a railway line, the face in the caption seemed vaguely familiar.'

'The mind playing tricks I expect with so many things happening. I mean take for an instance Mildred Marsh's cottage, all this time empty and neglected. It probably needs a good airing and the store closing with no sign of George McDonald, at least we know where he is now.'

'It's funny you should mention Mildred.' Ralph paused, for a moment deep in thought. 'The face in the caption,' he mumbled, 'No it can't be.'

'What dear, what did you say?' Maria started up the path.

'Nothing, just thinking aloud. But wait,' he grabbed her arm. 'There was something. Most of the time I was there George was incoherent but just as I was going he became quite lucid, although his voice was becoming weaker, drugs I suppose.'

'Did he say anything in particular?'

'Yes,' he uttered. 'Iris … Iris, I need a lawyer, get me a lawyer.' I said I would. Then as I told you, he smiled as I got up to leave.'

'You said he seemed a little confused on occasions, I wouldn't put much credence on that.' Maria picked up her gardening gloves and fork.

'But suppose it's genuine, a cry for help. I can't turn my back, I'd never forgive myself. Perhaps I'll call and see Iris, after all she's only across the road, on the pretext of a goodwill visit. I saw her out in the garden, earlier this morning while waiting for the bus; I don't think she saw me.'

'It's funny you should say that, I saw Charlie walking up the road with that dog, the other day, he'd looked like he'd been in the wars. The boy looked really down in the mouth. I hope every thing's alright. They'd appreciate a visit I'm sure. But not now, who's for a spot of lunch?' Maria tucked her arm in Ralph's. 'I've a hotpot in the oven with our own home grown peas and pota-toes. How about that? My, won't I be glad to take these boots off.'

CHAPTER 23

In a room, with the curtains partially drawn, Marco found himself in a tranquil ambience, so different to that of the hustle and bustle of the bright and airy corridor he had left behind. Shallow breathing emanated from a shadowy image in a bed near the window, intrigued he crept closer. A gentle breeze lifted the curtains shedding light on the facial features and form of a man. Marco stepped back, as muttering incoherently, the incumbent rolled over onto his side.

Earlier Marco lurking by the reception desk in the busy hospital foyer, had managed as far as he knew to remain inconspicuous. There he kept his ear to the ground, picking up any relevant information that came his way, the like of which had led him to the room where George McDonald lay. But where was Charlie? No matter what, this was no time to reflect for the next moment on hearing the echo of footsteps and ultimately a murmur of voices outside the door, in his haste to conceal himself, he knocked over a vase of flowers.

Marco gathered them up, and stuffed them back into the vase, with his handkerchief he mopped up a tell tale pool of water, crouching in the shadows, he hid behind a chair near to the door, with a view to beating a hasty retreat. The door swung open, revealing a group of people, all of whom to his relief were looking in the direction of the bed.

'So how is he?' asked a familiar voice. Marco peeped out. Charlie's mother now in the middle of the room was addressing a nurse, beside her, her husband and alongside him Charlie. Charlie appeared to be staring at the floor and then at the flowers he, Marco had so quickly retrieved.

'As well as can be expected,' said the nurse. 'It's amazing what a little rest can do, but it will take time. I gather he was asking for you, or so the Rev. Watson told me.'

'Asking for me, but why?' asked Iris, with a puzzled expression on her face.

'He didn't say,' said the nurse, crossing the room and drawing back the curtains. 'Maybe it's just the ramblings of a patient who cannot cope, but I gather Mr. McDonald was quite lucid at the time.' She glanced at her fob watch. 'I must be off. 'If you need any help, just press the bell.' The door closed behind her.

'Harry, what do you think of that?' Iris raised an enquiring eyebrow.

Harry shrugged his shoulders. 'How should I know? Why don't you ask the Vicar what it's all about, he's right on our doorstep.'

Iris moved closer to the bed. 'George, it's Iris, can you hear me?' Iris bending over the still figure could have sworn his lips moved. 'George it's Iris.' George's hand lay on the coverlet, Iris picked it up and held in hers. But she found no response in the contact, no warmth, to her it was limp and cold to the touch. She laid it down.

'Harry, we're wasting our time.' Iris turned to go. 'We could come another time, or ring and see how he is.'

'No give him a chance,' Harry stayed her arm. 'Perhaps he's not fully awake.' He drew up two chairs. 'Here come and sit by me. There's some magazines over there on that table.'

'Here, what's this?' Iris about to sit down glimpsed the crumpled newspaper on the floor. She picked it up and smoothed out the creases. 'It todays!' She caste it aside. 'It's of no use to me, I'll bin it. But what's this!' Iris had spotted the vase of flowers. 'Really Harry, you'd think they would be tastefully arranged.' She eyed them with distain. Taking out the flowers, she picked up the vase. 'Would you believe it,' she exclaimed, 'No water!' She stepped to a sink in a corner to turn on a tap. Seized by a thought, she swung around. 'These must have been the ones I saw the Vicar holding at the bus stop, I would never have believed it of him.'

Charlie up until now had been ignored. He had taken the seat near the door. He disliked hospitals; they smelt of disinfectant, of people dead or dying. He hadn't wanted to come in the first place. He wouldn't have, if it hadn't been for Rover. The dog, he liked to think of as his, had led him across fields, through hedgerows to the narrow country lane. There he had come across the green van and it's occupant. But where was Marco? Why had he run so far on ahead?

Silent and moody, Charlie fidgeted, his eyes fixed on the wall clock. To him the hands on the clock scarcely moved. A pile of magazines on a nearby table caught his eye, on the top of the pile a comic, 'The Dandy.' His spirits lifted but were soon dashed when he found he had read it.

Meanwhile, Marco in a quandary, hadn't expected to find himself in such close proximity to Charlie. He now found himself in an uncomfortable position, one that hadn't improved with time. The gypsy crouched at floor level with his nose almost touching the floorboards had watched Charlie's trainers on the move. The next moment, a comic presumably discarded by Charlie landed on the floor. Charlie's mother and father still engaged in conversation, Marco seeing this as a golden opportunity inched forward. On hands and knees, his vision restricted, edging his way around the arm of the chair, he whispered. 'Charlie … It's Marco, don' 'e look, act as if I ain't 'ere. Follow me, them's not lookin'.'

At the unexpected sound of Marco's voice, Charlie at first thought he was imagining things. But knowing Marco's volatile nature, knew him to be capable of anything. It was just like him to suddenly appear without any explanation. Charlie welcomed the diversion, for he was bored and wouldn't be missed.

As luck would have it the door ajar, they made good their escape. Down the corridor the two raced narrowly avoiding a nurse. Further along, they found an empty room. Marco dragged Charlie inside.

'Where 'ave 'e bin.' Charlie's eyes narrowed. 'Makin' off an' leavin me.'

Marco for once impressed, studied Charlie's face for any sign of weakness. 'Don' 'e know, us ain't 'anging' 'round fer 'e!'

'Cos I'm too slow, I suppose? Wot if I is.' Charlie hadn't expected an apology, but seized by a thought, asked. 'Wot's 'e doin' 'ere?'

Marco took a deep breath. 'After, … I left 'e,' he drawled in an attempt to impress. 'I found … this 'ere green van. The same one us saw that night leavin' the big 'ouse when us 'eard someone shoutin' 'elp. I knew I mustn't 'ang 'round bein' a gypo, it bein' the storekeeper. The place crawlin' with cops, they'd think I'd done 'im in, 'e bein' as dead as mutton. Now 'e knows.'

'I knows, I knew already. And 'e 'ain't dead, 'e's in 'ospital, as 'e knows.' Charlie was getting fed up with Marco's high handed attitude. 'Anyways I saw 'im meself. Took a lift in a police car too, me an' the dog.'

''e wot! 'e ain't spilt the beans.' Marco's eyes were like organ stops.

'Wot do 'e think?' Charlie eyed him disdainfully.

'The body on the line, suppose 'e's 'eard 'bout that.' Marco quickly changed the subject.

'I might 'ave.' Charlie was enjoying playing hard to get.

'Suppose I tells 'e somethin'. Suppose I tell 'e it wos that 'orrible woman.'

'Mildred Marsh!' The penny dropped, aghast, Charlie asked. 'ow do 'e know?'

'Cos I wos there.' Marco smirked.

'You'm tellin' fibs.'

'Ain't! Us 'elp this man find 'e's dog. The dog found 'er, 'er wos covered in blood, 'er wos a mess. Wait till I tells Mario.' Marco chortled. 'e never liked 'er!'

An echo of footsteps and hollow voices in the corridor brought the conversation to an abrupt end. 'Us mustn't be found 'ere.' Marco wide-eyed stood by the door as if taking flight. Best be goin' while the coast's clear. But afore I do, there's somethin' else, a bunch of violets…' Marco opened the door a crack and peered out.

'A bunch of violets, wot 'bout 'em?' Charlie frowned. To this there was no reply for Marco like the bird had flown.

❧

CHAPTER 24

Murder!' Mildred Marsh?' Maria, the Vicar wife, stunned by the news, sinking back in her chair, gripped the arm rests.

Ralph nodded. 'They are reopening the case. There's going to be a post mortem.'

'Who would want to murder her? I know she wasn't liked.' Her eyes widened. 'Ralph, do you think she had it coming to her?'

Ralph looked grave. 'She was a regular churchgoer. It's not my place to judge.'

'So you've nothing to say. But you should, as a man of the cloth. It's part of your job to reach out to others in need, in times of adversity, isn't it? Maria raised a questioning eyebrow; her hazel brown eyes searched his face for an answer.

Ralph struggled with his conscience. Should he have something to say? Was it expected of him? 'I've been thinking.' Deep in thought, he sat doodling on a scrap of paper. 'About the time …'

'Yes,' Maria leant forward all ears.

'About the time I overheard her telling off the gypsy on the church steps. Do you think it's relevant?'

'Really Ralph, it's just an isolated incident. She was known to have a sharp tongue. It was her way.' Maria frowned. 'Was there any sign of violence?'

'No, I saw her the very next moment, she seemed agitated, she wasn't wearing stockings, I thought that strange. That wasn't like her. But when I asked her if she was alright, she said she was and I wasn't to worry. That was the last time I saw her.'

Yes, she was a woman a person couldn't get close to, a very strange woman. I wonder …' Maria stared pensively into space. 'And George McDonald, he's another one. He and Mildred disappeared at roughly the same time, I wonder if there's any connection.'

Ralph adjusted his dog collar and leant back in his chair. 'Yesterday,' he said, his eyes alighting on a straying spider, 'I took a stroll through the village, put my ear to the ground. The news on the broadsheet was on everyone's lips, accusing fingers pointed at the empty store. A general feeling of disquiet prevailed.' Again Ralph wondered, should he have said something? Given some crumbs of comfort. Was it expected of him? A special service in the church? A meeting in the village hall?

'And Emily, what about Emily?' Maria broke a prolonged silence.

'Poor Emily, I saw her on my rounds. The closing of the store has robbed her of her independence. Now she takes a taxi to Chillingford, other times with Harold and Iris in the car. She's a frail old lady not only can she ill afford the taxi, the journey tires her.'

'She was pleased with the fresh veg from our plot.' Maria's face lit up. 'It was nice to see a smile on her face. Then she tells me, 'I mustn't do it again. She's so stubborn.' Maria sighed. 'Will George ever come back, will he ever reopen the shop? I hope so.'

෧ඪල

CHAPTER 25

'The body on the railway line. Any bright ideas, Blackley?' Inspector Charles Routley's eyes teased. 'The note on the body for an instance. Could it have been planted by persons unknown?'

'I don't know Sir,' Constable Edward Blackley hovering by the desk, coughed nervously. Routley was in one of his cat and mouse moods and he didn't want to be the prey.

'Could the deceased have not been involved with the burglary and subsequent brutal attack at the Gables?' The Inspector's sharp eyes scanned Blackley's face.

The young constable flushed. Why ask him? There were others on the case, Routley knew that.

'You'll never make a policeman.' Routley drained his coffee cup. He handed it to Blackley who placed it on a tray. 'Although I've been known to be wrong.' He smiled condescendingly. 'And you make a good cup of coffee, if and when I get it.'

Blackley mustered up a smile. 'Can I go Sir?'

Routley nodded, lent back in his chair and closed his eyes. Since finding the body on the railway track, things had gone quiet. On the surface with the findings of the post mortem, the case had at first seemed straight forward, but now he was beginning to have his doubts. He would have liked to think so but knew there wasn't such a thing as an easy answer. There was bound to be a snag somewhere along the line. Too many things had happened, too much water gone under the bridge.

Someone somewhere held the key. But who? If anyone, Nettlebridge's village policeman, Constable Robbie Phillips? After all he was on the spot. He recalled a phone call made not so long ago to break the news about the missing storekeeper. Phillips at the time had already known about the discovery of the green van and its occupant in a country lane just outside Nettlebridge, but had failed to inform him due to a breakdown of communication. The presence of a boy? What boy? Phillips had had no idea what he was talking about.

Constables Perkins and Harris had. They had found him dirty, tired and distraught on a road not far from Chillingford hospital, padding by his side an unkempt mongrel. On their approach the boy collapsed. He had refused point blank, the suggestion of an ambulance. They had carried him to the patrol car. 'Leave me dog and me alone,' he said. 'I 'ain't ill. I wanna go 'ome, 'till I find Marco that is. But where's me friend gone?'

Marco, a strange name. A name that still preyed on Routley's mind. Mysteries frustrated him, particularly unsolved ones. It must be the name of one of those gypsies. Had Phillips picked up any clues at their encampment when on a good will visit? He should have heard by now.

Routley got up, and stepped to the window sill. Nothing much to see. A solitary figure standing on the hump back bridge feeding the ducks, other than that a quiet grey day with glimpses of the sun. The car park empty, Perkins and Harrison out on traffic control, should have been back by now. Wherever were they?

CHAPTER 26

George McDonald stretched and yawned as standing outside his store in the fading light. Discharged from the hospital he now hoped to put the past behind him. It had not been the homecoming he would have liked. The shop-front grimy, the paint peeling, emptied of stock, tomorrow at the crack of dawn with a pan and brush, and a bucketful of soapy water, he resolved to work with a will. He caste a cursory glance up and down the fore-street. Come to think of it the village itself looked rundown, or was it the misty rain and the grey sky, whatever it was, it mirrored his mood.

The lights in the Blue Boar down the road having just gone on, cast a cheery glow on the dampened pavements. He heard loud voices and the slamming of doors. A stocky figure emerging stood on the pavement. In the gloom it appeared to be that of Harry Blackmore. Harry glanced in George's direction, then after a second look, with an air of assurance taking long strides down the road drew abreast.

'I thought it was you. Glad to see you back in the land of living, George.'

'Glad to be back. How's Iris and the boy?' Harry's voice slurred, George smelled alcohol on his breath. He was tempted to say, 'It's a bit early for that,' but changed his mind.

'Don't ask.' Harry frowned. 'Charlie's taken to making off. Iris is at her wits end. She blames me.'

Who really is to blame? George pondered. He envied Harry, would have liked to have been in his shoes. He quelled a strong desire to interfere. It was not his place to do so. Had his mother not put her spoke in it, would he have coped? He would never know.

'I suppose you haven't heard.' Harry broke an awkward silence.

'Heard what?'

Mildred Marsh has been found dead on the railway line just outside Nettlebridge. It's in all the papers. A note was found on her body. It's thought she committed suicide. Her cottage is going to wrack and ruin. Good riddance to bad rubbish, that's what I say!' At that moment, the church clock chimed the hour. George glanced at his watch, his eyes widened. 'Cor blimey, is it that time already. I'd best be on my way, else I'll get a right ticking off.'

George watching Harry's shambling gait with a sense of remorse, wondered what the future held for Iris and Charlie. He hoped it bode good.

Alone again, George mused. The Vicar on a visit to the hospital had brought the day's newspaper, which he had left neatly folded by his bed. He'd reached out and picked it up with the intention of reading it. A woman's body had been found on a railway line just outside Nettlebridge. So close to home, his interest aroused, he read on. He studied the caption and the woman's face, although bloodied and almost unrecognisable, he could have sworn he had seen it before. But where and when? His mind in a fog at the time, he had a job to remember anything, added to which the nurse catching him reading the caption had taken it away.

So that's who it was, now he knew.

Mildred may have taken the easy way out, leaving him in the cart. A note had been found near the body. What was in it? A dark thought occurred. Had she spilt the beans?

An air of gloom clouded his mind.

A clip clop of horse's hooves brought him back to a stark reality. 'Nice to see you back, with the old post office shut down and a dwindling supply of meat with Amos Higgin's shop on the market, things are coming to a pretty pass.' Helen Ferris who mucked out the stables at the Riding School on the outskirts of the village was exercising Dusty, a silvery grey mare. The mare threw back her head as she drew up and neighed. Helen giggled. 'It seems as if she's in agreement. She patted Dusty's steaming flank. 'There will be a carrot or two when I'm passing this way, I guess.'

'Probably, once I get my house in order.' George smiled up at the fair-haired girl. 'I must say, it will be nice to be back in the old routine. Let's hope the weather picks up, it makes all the difference. Mind how you go down Deep Hole Lane it's a known black spot and with this misty rain it could be slippery, looks like we've seen the last of summer.'

In response, Helen pulled a face and rode away.

The discourse and unaccustomed banter lifted George's spirits. He was back where he belonged. But things had changed and not always for the better. The Post Office so long a part of the fore street, now empty devoid of life, a sad reflection of what had been. Straight laced, Miriam Peters the postmistress, always to be found behind the counter, there no more. He like so many others would miss her and her quiet ways. Where had she gone and why? The news had come as a shock, so immersed in his own problems he hadn't even been aware of what was going on. Who would take her place? He wondered. And when?

Before stepping inside, a creature of habit George rubbed a grimy side window with his pocket handkerchief. One of the notices pinned on the board inside was missing. Which one was that? Then it came to him, how could he have forgotten, the words in large black capitals, NO GYPSIES SERVED HERE, he had found so soul destroying, in his rage, he had torn it up in little pieces and thrown it away. His eyes filled with tears of remorse. The words had brought a range of emotions. He neither despised nor cared about the gypsies. To him personally in their encampment outside the village they held no threat, but pressure had been brought to bear above all by Mildred Marsh.

Emily got off the bus. It had been a long and tiring day. A bumpy ride from Chillingford, her bones ached, her corns were playing up with the drag about town. She raised her umbrella, the thick drizzle penetrating her thick skirt and dirtying her lace up shoes, she had not dressed for a rainy day. Before making her way home, she stopped and stared. Her old eyes drawn to a young girl seated on horse outside the village store, she wondered who she was talking to. She adjusted her glasses. Her face relaxed at a thought, her thin lips parted in a smile. George is back, she breathed. Thank God, now I won't have so far to go. Consoled by the thought, she humped her loaded basket down the road, a trying day like this she could now put behind her.

∽⊙∾

CHAPTER 27

On the river bank, Mario in a cold sweat awoke with a start from a nightmare. Whose going to believe you! A gypsy! Give yourself up. Mildred Marsh's taunting voice still rang in his ears. Once again in his dream, as in real life he had found himself on the church steps lost for words. As a gypsy, he had lost face, she had humiliated him. A proud man, he would never live it down. He felt a sense of remorse.

Stiff in his joints, wearily he struggled to his feet. Even the countryside he loved spread out before him, basking in the last rays of the setting sun failed to lift his spirits. A wind picking up, rippling the waters of the stream, his makeshift fire burnt to cinders, his mind wandered once again to that of a Bohemian Summer now coming to an end. The cries of birds winging home to their nests told him this in no uncertain terms. Any moment now they would take a series of practiced runs before taking to the air to their wintering grounds, far, far away. Soon the fields and hedgerows would be carpeted with a thin layer of frost and in time the air filled with flurries of snow, for him too it was time to move on.

Where's that boy?' Mario frustrated, envisaged a belligerent Eliza and the lash of her tongue. How like Marco to make off leaving him to carry the can. If Eliza found out Marco was again with that village boy, his Mario's life wouldn't be worth living. He vaguely remembered gunfire, it must have frightened the dog, he supposed, not surprising since the poor thing having been peppered with shots by an irate farmer, had been lucky to escape with its life. At peace with the world, it had been laying in-front of the fire.

'I'm not waitin' 'round 'ere fer 'em, I knows that much. But wot am I goin' to tell Eliza?' He shrugged his shoulders. ''ers bound to ask questions.'

Mario straightening his tattered cap, picked up his tackle and made for the edge of the woods. There he stood as before beneath the trees puffing away at his pipe, picturing the spot where not so long ago he and Marco had spotted Charlie. The field then blanketed in a heat haze, clearly now lifted, so different in the fading light. He turned away. Like it or not he would have to make his own way back to the encampment. He didn't relish the idea, but under the circumstances thought, needs must if the devil drives. On the other hand if he brought home say a rabbit for a pie as a peace offering that would make a difference. No sooner had the thought occurred than he heard the sharp throaty cry of a pheasant. A bar of sunlit glancing off a tree trunk outlined it's showy image. He levelled his shot gun and fired. This time the prize would be his not the dogs.

Sure of his aim, he stepped to the spot. It lay where it fell, a colourful trophy. Mario when picking it up, although hardened to the chase, as usual felt an initial sadness. A tender spot for all living creatures, an emotion the laws of nature deemed impractical, once again he'd have to dismiss such feelings out of hand.

Finding his way back along the rough woodland track in the soft dim light, Mario paused on seeing again the putrid pool, to him a murky mini swamp. Rotten and foul it may be, but to the flies and insects buzzing around it's green slimy surface, their little world.

Nearby a squirrel out nutting fearful of Mario's heavy tread shinned up a gnarled trunk to a leafy shelter. At the sight, Mario's face broke into a smile. 'Enterprising little fellows,' he muttered aloud. 'Busy bees!' A rabbit as industrious, some way ahead, squat on it hind legs cleaning its whiskered face. Forewarned, as fast as a streak of lightening it's white powder puff tail bobbing, it leapt into a tangle of undergrowth.

Birds chirped, bees hummed, Mario picking his way, stopped now and then to relish nature's harmony.

'Nearly there.' He muttered, sometime later. The trees thinning, coming to the edge of the wood, he waded across the slow flowing stream, then past a number of horses cropping on it's banks. The field quiet, but for a number of lamp lit wagons in the encampment, no-one appeared to be around. Eliza out and about? He stepped closer to get a better look. There was no sign of her, nor any lamplight in the wagon. From his waistcoat pocket he withdrew his pocket watch and snapped it open. It's hands pointed to ten o'clock. Eliza must have gone to bed. Mario not wanting to draw attention to himself crept across the field. Even the dogs asleep inside the farm gate hadn't stirred on his approach. As luck would have it, Lorenzo, his next door neighbour was outside his caravan shoeing his long suffering horse. A buddy of long standing, he looked up on hearing the crunch of Mario's heavy boots. 'Oh it's you.' He gave a crafty smile. Where's the boy? Lost 'm again?'

'ow should I know where 'e gits to.' Mario felt grumpy. 'e's a mind of his own 'ain't 'e?'

'Suppose so, but yer ole woman don' see it that way, by wot 'er's bin sayin'. He clapped Mario on the back. 'I don' envy 'e.'

'So wot!' Mario mustered up a smile. 'I've got a peace offerin ...' He held up the pheasant.

'T'will do fer a time I suppose, til 'er starts to think.' Lorenzo having shoed the roan, patted it's rump. 'I wouldna like to be in your shoes ... boots.'

'Wouldn' 'e? ...'ow's that?'

'Now yer Marco's made off wi' Charlie.'

'How did 'e know that?' Mario was flabbergasted. 'ho told 'e?'

'I knows, cos 'es like you, won' be beaten.' Lorenzo gave a sickly grin.

'Stop yer soft soapin'. If 'e wants to borra money I ain't got any.' Mario wasn't going to be thought a fool, least of all now.

'Haven't 'e, that's not wot I've 'eard. Still when 'e 'ave a mind. Till then, got to go, me suppers on the table, us be 'aving it in the wagon, tis warmer.'

Mario all on his own didn't know what to think. 'What had Eliza been saying? Had she like Lorenzo put two and two together and made four?

❧

CHAPTER 28

The Inspector rose from his desk. He stood by the window sill and looked out. The weather on the turn with a pale sky and the proverbial misty rain, he envisaged a dreary aspect. Over the humped backed bridge, a mushrooming of umbrellas, along the high street a herd of cows playing follow my leader to market, a watchful dog in tow. Only the ducks were happy in their watery playground.

A discreet knock at the door, he bellowed, 'Who is it? Come in.'

The door swung open to admit a tentative Blackley. 'Your morning coffee, Sir.'

'How many more times?' Routley red in the face, thumped the desk with his fist. 'I want tea not coffee. Take it away!'

'Sorry Sir ... shall I? Blackley's hand shook, the coffee slopping into the saucer.

'You heard what I said, take it away!'

The door slammed shut.

Routley sat down heavily; the chair creaked under his weight. He ruffled the papers in front of him. Doodling on a notebook, he surmised. As he'd thought the affair at the Gables a complicated case, it being long and drawn out. An Inspector's nightmare with no light at the end of the tunnel. A number of probable suspects but without any proof, no conviction.

Mrs Symons, the Colonel's housekeeper in her statement had alluded to the Colonel's dislike of the gypsies. But there were a number of others in the village who shared his opinion. And visa versa when Phillips, the village policeman had visited the encampment, there had been no love lost.

The gypsy boy who'd rammed on the police house door on the night of the incident had said there'd been a murder at the Gables. Had that been Marco? The same name kept cropping up in the course of his investigation. Charlie the village boy when questioned had mentioned a boy named Marco. And what about the green van seen on the night of the robbery driven away at speed? Had it been George McDonald's or another van? If George McDonald's, had he been behind the wheel or someone else? Viewed at a distance not far from the boundary wall, the sole witnesses, Charlie and presumably this Marco hadn't been sure.

Not long after the event, the Vicar had overheard an heated argument between Mildred Marsh and a gypsy on the church steps. According to the Rev Ralph Watson the verbal onslaught had become violent. The assailant he thought Mildred Marsh although he couldn't be sure.

What had the gypsy been doing there in the first place? When questioned at the gypsy encampment Mario in his defence had said that he only wanted to know where the Police House was. His name Mario, Marco, his son had told him about the gent who lived in the big house, that he and the village boy had heard cries and shouts for help. His son at the time, him being a gypsy thought he may well have been accused of being involved. Fearful he had run away leaving his friend behind. Marco when questioned separately about his movements, had said the self same thing. Where they colluding?

And what about the victim? Colonel Clifford Hardwick having come out of his coma, had said it was Mildred Marsh who attacked him. Had there been someone else with her? The Colonel when asked, hadn't been sure, although there might have been. He said he had heard voices just before losing consciousness.

Perkins and Harrison out on patrol had radioed in to say they had found a green van in a lane just outside Nettlebridge. George McDonald inside slumped over the steering wheel in what they had thought a drunken stupor. Not long after when following the ambulance they had picked up a boy with a dog. The boy had said he wanted to go home and where was Marco?

The same green van as that on the night of the robbery?' Routley frowned. The boy with a dog, could it have been Charlie?

The lost dog, the body on the railway line. Marco's account of what happened. There again the gypsy boy hadn't wanted to be involve and had left the scene, but not before drawing attention to a bunch of violets.

A message had been found inside the wrapper. A statement in block capitals written and presumably signed by a Mildred Marsh saying she and she alone was the sole perpetrator of the crime. Routley had found this hard to believe.

A middle-aged woman, overweight from what he'd envisaged capable of committing such a violent assault on a frail old man. It beggared believe. Had she committed suicide or was she pushed? Had she been forced to write the note beforehand?

George McDonald, the proprietor of the Nettlebridge Stores, he'd heard tell had shut up shop for no apparent reason and simply disappeared. The only rational explanation having been that due to the sudden death of his mother he had suffered a nervous breakdown.

Routley leant back in his chair and closed his eyes. It was down to him, should he close a case with no leads? If so, like so many others unresolved it would lie festering in the filing cabinet, never to see the light of day. That wouldn't do. Why not throw it open, let others decide, as in time, no doubt others would. With this thought in mind, in due course, he was to find the case he'd thought so complicated had by all intents and purposes been thought by others as clear cut.

Brought to court, the jury in their wisdom, had unanimously agreed, that Mildred Marsh had taken her own life when the balance of her mind was disturbed.

CHAPTER 29

Word got out, the news travelled like wild fire from the village to the gypsy encampment, the case hyped by the media. The Nettlebridge Stores this time with a newly acquired Post Office had once again become a hot bed of gossip, Amos Higgins, the butcher, his shop on the mend, his old congenial self.

'Shame about the Gables,' folks were heard to say. 'A place like that left to go to rack and ruin. Perhaps a use will be found for it in time, when the Colonel's up and about again. And to think the old man would want to live in Mildred's old cottage with all it's ghosts, and that loot still up in the loft. Still he's got his housekeeper at hand. She devoted to him, although there's not much for her to do.'

The gypsies absorbed from all blame, now freer in movement, wandered at will through the village, watched by villagers. Over tankards of beer in the Blue Boar, tongues wagged at such a spectacle, each and everyone suspicious and unsure of the outcome. The travellers too, aware of a certain amount of hostility guarded their tongues. But in time given the chance, purely down to the Vicar had found a way to mix, and make friends with some, albeit on a tentative basis.

Iris one memorable afternoon out in the garden dead heading her roses, spotted Mario purposely making his way in her direction. She felt slightly intimidated by what she considered his fearsome appearance. What did he want? She had nothing to sell. No unwanted disused household articles. He would have to try elsewhere.

Catching sight of her, Mario gave a toothless grin and raised his cap. 'Would Mister Harry like to go fishin'?' He boomed, drawing abreast.

Iris felt tickled pink.

'I don't think so. My husbands at work.' A thought occurred. And even if he wasn't, he hasn't got a fishing permit. 'It's Mario, Marco's father isn't it,' Iris mustered up a smile. 'I don't think we've met.' She held out her hand.

He took it in his rough calloused one and shook it vigorously. 'Well I'll be off then,' he said. 'Mustn't keep the fish waitin.'

❧

CHAPTER 30

'Ma where are you?'

'Up in the loft, I'm having a clearout, if you're coming up, mind how you go, that stepladders had it's day, it's infested with woodwork. Ah, there you are,' Iris straightened herself up, as Charlie sticking his head through the narrow aperture, clambered up onto the dusty floor boards to join her.

'I was wondering where you were.' She glanced at her watch. 'You should have been home from school, over an hour ago, where have you been?'

'Bin down to see me mate, Marco.'

'Again!' Charlie you know I don't like you being out on your own, now the evenings are drawing in. I told you to come straight home. Although, if I'd known it, I could have given you some caste offs for the gypsies.'

'But Ma, I 'ave to go, I 'ave to see Marco. 'e told me, them's gettin' ready fer the road, then 'e won be 'round anymore.' Charlie's eyes lost their sparkle. 'Then wot am I goin' to do?'

'You've got Rover. He's been making hell of a racket, tied up out there in the backyard.'

'I best come an' git'im, I suppose next time.' Charlie gaped. 'Ma, you'm not gittin' rid of me Action Man.'

'You never look at it, it's up here gathering dust and cobwebs.' As if on cue, a spider with long hairy legs, it's tranquil life disturbed, raced over long forgotten toys, books, old lampshades, and a bicycle pump. Iris, her dark hair protected by a paisley scarf, squeamish, cringed.

'I'll git rid.' Charlie scooped the offending creature up in a handkerchief, and popped it out the open skylight.

On her hands and knees, in the process of packing all manner of things into a large box, Iris came across a 1930s radio. She twiddled the knobs, 'Not a peep, what a shame, it could have been a talking point.'

'Who wants to talk 'bout that?' Charlie wasn't impressed. 'That's borin'.

'I wouldn't expect you to be interested,' Iris said, 'you weren't even born. But where did it come from, that's what I want to know?'

Turning her attention to personal effects, her eyes rested on holiday snaps with the girls at work, her whirlwind romance and wedding to Harry in the church across the way, another of Charlie, a chubby cheeked three year old riding Neddy. 'Do you want to keep Neddy?' The wooden rocking horse, much the worse for wear stood in a corner, like everything else abandoned, as the stepladder, probably infested with wood worm.

Charlie shook his head. 'Wot's this?' Sinking to his knees, he picked up a crumpled black and white photograph.

'What's that doing there on the floor? It must have fallen out of the album.' Puzzled, Iris took it from him and dusted it off.

'Can I 'ave a butchers?' Charlie took a look. He sniggered. 'Mr McDonald wi' a lot more 'air. 'ow did 'e get that?'

'I don't know.' Iris frowned. 'I shall have to hand it back.'

❧

'What's wrong, Iris? I haven't slept a wink. You've been twisting and turning all night.' Harry glanced at the illuminated dial. 'Half five, I should be gone within the hour. Switching on the lamp, he sat up and rubbed his eyes. 'They're short of man power at the saw mill, more money in me pay packet I suppose, but hard going. Well, what's on your mind?'

'Nothing really.' Iris yawned. Nothing but a dream or a nightmare, but it was so real, it was if I was there. A sudden impact, a screech of brakes, a soft bed of grass on a roadside verge, and a voice, telling me 'You'll be alright, over and over again.'

'My voice, I suppose.' Harry, fully clothed, stepped towards the door.

'No strangely enough, not yours but someone else's.' Iris sitting up in bed, clutched hold of her knees.'

'Whose?'

'Would you believe it, George McDonald's it doesn't make sense. I must be imagining things. I found a photo, yesterday afternoon in the loft, while you were at work, a photo of a young George McDonald.' The words came out in a rush.

'And …' Harry raised an eyebrow.

'For some reason, I can't get it out of my mind.'

'Iris … I've got to go else I'll be late for work, but there's something you should know.'

'Oh, what's that?'

'I can't tell you now. It will have to keep until tonight.'

❦

George McDonald out the back rearranging the stock, heard the shop bell, straightening his apron, he stepped out to see who it was.

Iris stood just inside the door.

'Iris, what can I do for you?' His eyes searched her face.

Generally never short for words, pale faced, she hovered on the spot, her eyes downcast.

'Is something wrong?' George moved out from behind the counter.

She clicked open her handbag, took out and handed him the photo. 'I thought you should have this.' Slightly out of her depth, she blushed. 'I found it up in the loft; goodness knows how it got there.'

George's lack of response, when looking at it puzzled her. For a while, he remained silent, sombre eyed.

She stepped aside, as approaching the shop door, he turned the sign to 'Closed.' He stood back and faced her a serious expression on his face. Subdued, he uttered. 'There's something you should know.'

'That's what Harry said, if this is some sort of prank.' Iris felt a tightening of the throat. 'I'm not amused.'

'Iris prepare yourself for a shock.'

'Prepare, myself for a shock! What shock? What are you trying to tell me? You're not making sense.' Iris, her heart thumping in her chest, wondered what he was going to say next.

'Charlie, is our son … yours and mine.' George having thought of himself saying this so many times, now having said it, was lost for words.

'You're joking!' Iris holding his gaze couldn't even detect a glimmer of a smile. 'You are aren't you?'

'No, I wish I was, it would have saved a lot of heartache all around.' George having said this, felt a tremendous sense of relief.

'What heartache, what's this all about?' Iris cried, fearful, with an impending sense of doom. In a quandary, she had not as yet grasped the significance of George's revelation if true, or of it's potential impact on her life.

Aware of this, George offering a steadying arm guided her into a cosy back room.

Over a cups of hot strong tea, and biscuits, he bared his heart, Iris at first sceptical, then a wrapt audience, glued to her seat. He told her of his mother's bitterness, how as an only child, she had controlled him, and as a man had continued to do so, of her husband, his father leaving her for another woman.

'And then I met you and fell in love.' His lips trembled. 'And what happened then?' Iris asked, a thought occurred. 'Don't tell me, I'm beginning to see the light.' She told him there and then about the dream, George filling in the gaps. It was as if awakening from a long sleep.

'That's exactly how it happened; I didn't know what to do at the time. Now you know.' George drained of all emotion, sunk back in his chair.

Iris gave a sympathetic smile. 'Just like Mildred Marsh, your mother was a very nasty woman.'

Her unexpected remark, had set him thinking, suspicious, he asked. 'What makes you say that?'

'The robbery at the Gables, you were involved weren't you?'

George was taken aback.

'Iris gave a sly smile. 'I'm right aren't I? You shut up shop without any explanation, it wasn't like you, and like her you couldn't be found anywhere. It was too much of a coincidence.'

'You're quite the little detective, aren't you?' George mustered up a smile.

'I'm logical I grant you that. So where do we go from here?'

'Will I be put behind bars?'

She shook her head. 'I shan't tell a soul, although Charlie will have to be told that you're his father.' She hesitated. 'You could tell him yourself in your own time. It will come as a shock. But he's young, he'll adapt, and will get used to you being around, that's if … you're staying.'

'And Harry?' George raised a questioning eyebrow. 'Where does he come into it?'

'Harry knows, he's always known, I should have twigged that this morning. He must have simply filled the breach when you left me. We're a happy family unit now and I want to keep it that way, and with a little bit of luck another one on the way. Harry doesn't know yet, I've only just found out myself. And you George what will you do?'

'Nothing much.' George searched for words. 'I'll stay as I am. Can you ever forgive me?'

'There's nothing to forgive.' Iris picked up her handbag and made for the door. She turned and smiled, before lifting the latch. 'And I really mean that.'

∽⌾∾

CHAPTER 31

The venue fixed, a meeting held, a decision made, now a hubbub of activity in the encampment with gypsies on the move. With darker evenings, the onset of winter and snow in the air, many are raring to go. Mario and Lorenzo amongst others, spending daylight hours, hunting and fishing, with a need to replenish their larders.

Marco and Charlie with Rover, now roaming at random through glades of reddish brown leaves. An autumnal wonderland of blackberries ripe for the picking, with mushrooms almost the size of saucers soon to be laid amongst other fruits inside the church, on the altar steps. A cooler atmosphere with a smell of bonfires, mellow before the harsh realities of winter with storms like the howling of a hundred wolf packs.

'We plough the fields and scatter.' The church ringing with voices, Mario passing at the time, moved by so many memories, found himself dropping a brace of pheasants on the church steps, as a gesture of goodwill.

Marco with mixed feelings knows he will miss his friend, although they are worlds apart. On condition Mario walks Charlie home, Iris accepts Charlie's gypsy friend, knowing well that time is running out.

Many an evening until the early hours, under a harvest moon, the boys can be found sitting cross-legged in the firelight, listening to the emotive sounds of a fiddle.

Charlie spellbound, with gypsies singing traditional melodies, some happy, some sad, his eyes misting over with thoughts of a long lost summer, of the woods through which he, Marco and Mario had wandered, woods that once echoed with the sounds of wildlife, now a ghostly inhospitable place preparing for the onslaught of winter blasts.

Nature has spoken; the golden days have gone, urging the likes of Mario and Lorenzo and others to move on to pastures new before the roads and lanes become impassable.

In the gypsy camp, a carefree atmosphere, with expectations of the open road. A warm hazy glow with laughter and merriment, with women spreading clothes on bushes to air for the morrow.

Flanks groomed, manes and tails combed, hooves and harnesses checked, brasses buffed, in the fading light, horses and ponies, feed off bundles of hay, bantams cluck and scratch amongst sparse clumps of grass.

Shadowy figures grouped around fires, share their thoughts, feelings and hopes for the future, dogs at their feet, lying eyes shut, close to the flames.

A snapshot of contentment, never to be recaptured, just like the Colonel's memories, with it's passing nothing but a dream.

∽≈≈∽

A grey sky in late November, signals the very end of a Bohemian Summer. Lights blaze from cottages, wispy grey fingers of smoke from chimneys curl in a frosty atmosphere. With the first flurries of snow, this, a picture post card scene of the village of Nettlebridge at the turn of the year.

The air peppered with snowflakes, a stately procession trundles through the narrow fore street. Wagons, traps, trolleys, and carts packed to the gunnels, drawn by horses, cobs, piebalds, and ponies, chilled to the bone, snorting, their breath streaming in the cold crisp air. Bringing up the rear, packs of dogs, all shapes and sizes, barking excitedly, each vying to be first. The icy pavements on either side, thronged with villagers, blue with the cold, muffled, some with a heavy heart coming to wave goodbye, others merely to watch.

Leading the way, Mario at the reins, a clay pipe clenched in his mouth, stares fixedly ahead as the horse plods on, Amigo, his bright eyed terrier, sprawled on the footboard, watching his every move.

Clad in an old woollen overcoat, his cap set at a rakish angle, his dark eyes sombre, the Romany shows little emotion, his mind now fixed on another place, another time. Seated beside him, Marco in a threadbare coat scans the pavements and side lanes for a last glimpse of Charlie, his eyes lighting up when seeing him. Charlie at the cottage gate, waves a tearful goodbye, by his side, Rover barks and wags his tail in recognition, Amigo not to be outdone, barks in response.

In time, the wagon train but a spec in the distance, the cottagers disperse. The village as quiet as a graveyard, Charlie dries his eyes. No more will he see Marco, once, but only once, he would make his way back to the field, there to recapture a way of life, soon to become nothing but a memory.

∞≈∞

A grey sky with whitish cloud cover, interspersed with a blush of pink, sets the scene.

Charlie having reached the farm gate, fully expects to be met with a crescendo of barks. Marco's voice comes to mind. 'Them's only dogs there's plenty where they comes from.'

The field lies empty and deserted under a thin layer of snow, a heap of rubbish, speckled white, dumped at the foot of a tree. Bicycle parts, empty beer bottles, a discarded pram, redundant kitchen utensils, rusty wire netting, and amongst other things, a wagon wheel that has seen better days, the only signs of a once living, breathing community.

A wind picking up, with Rover at his heels, Charlie, his breath clouding the air, crunches over crisp grass, across the field to the spot where Marco's wagon had lain. The very spot where he, Mario and Marco had brought the injured dog, now his dog on that very first day. The dog he will call Rebel not Rover for as Marco had said it was his dog now.

There by the charred circle where a fire had been extinguished, he wallows in a silent world of faces and people peculiar to him, in a place where just a while ago, still visible, with an imprint of horse's hooves, and ruts in the muddied snow, wheels had turned.

A robin perched on an overhanging branch eyes him speculatively. Rebel barks, with a flurry of wings the redbreast takes to the air.

'Time to go home Charlie says, 'I's 'ungry, 'ain't you?'

❦

A HEART FOR AUTHORS À L'ÉCOUTE DES AUTEURS MIA ΚΑΡΔΙΑ ΓΙΑ ΣΥΓ
FÖR FÖRFATTARE UN CORAZÓN POR LOS AUTORES YAZARLARIMIZA GÖNÜL VERELİM S
PER AUTORI ET HJERTE FOR FORFATTERE EEN HART VOOR SCHRIJVERS TEMOS OS AU
ZINKERT SERCE DLA AUTORÓW EIN HERZ FÜR AUTOREN A HEART FOR AUTHORS À L'ÉCC
ВСЕЙ ДУШОЙ К АВТОРАМ ETT HJÄRTA FÖR FÖRFATTARE Á LA ESCUCHA DE LOS AUT
ΓΙΑ ΣΥΓΓΡΑΦΕΙΣ UN CUORE PER AUTORI ET HJERTE FOR FORFATTERE EE

The author

Janice Hutchings, spent her childhood in Oreston,
a small waterside village, on the shores of the
river Plym. Educated at Oreston Primary School,
Plymstock Secondary Modern School, she then at-
tended St. Dunstan Abbey for girls. In 1957, having
qualified as a shorthand typist, she was employed
by a number of companies until 1973, after which
she worked in a Charity shop from 1974 to 1981.
Inspired by her mother, a freelance journalist,
Janice embarked on a writing career. She has
written a number of short stories, some of which
have been published in "Countryside Tales". She is
the secretary of a Local Writers' Group. Her writing
venture, "Bohemian Summer" is her first book.
Other than writing, she loves rambling, walking her
dog and riding her motorcycle.

The publisher

*Whoever stops
getting better,
will in time stop
being good.*

This is the motto of novum publishing, and our focus
is on finding new manuscripts, publishing them and
offering long-term support to the authors.
Our publishing house was founded in 1997, and since
then it has become THE expert for new authors and
has won numerous awards.

**Our editorial team will peruse each manuscript
within a few weeks free of charge and without
obligation.**

You will find more information about
novum publishing and our books on the internet:

www.novum-publishing.co.uk

Lightning Source UK Ltd.
Milton Keynes UK
UKOW02f1542250516

274969UK00001B/21/P